"I've never seen Morgan so angry—"

Jassy stopped, swallowing convulsively. "But it's worse than that. He...he said that if I saw you again he'd.... Oh, it doesn't matter. He's fixed the date for my wedding to René," she finished flatly.

Max drew a long harsh breath. "Without telling you?"

"Yes. I keep telling him I won't marry René, but he takes no notice. Morgan can't care for me if he's willing to force me into a loveless marriage, can he? I'm just a business asset to him," she said miserably, her eyes filling with tears.

Max's arms tightened around her, offering comfort. "He can't force you to marry against your will," he said, and in that same deadly voice, "And so help me, I'll kill him with my bare hands if he even tries."

PATRICIA LAKE
is also the author of these

Harlequin Presents

465—UNTAMED WITCH
501—PERFECT PASSION

PATRICIA LAKE

wipe away the tears

Harlequin Books

TORONTO • LONDON • LOS ANGELES • AMSTERDAM
SYDNEY • HAMBURG • PARIS • STOCKHOLM • ATHENS • TOKYO

Harlequin Presents first edition August 1982
ISBN 0-373-10521-5

Original hardcover edition published in 1982
by Mills & Boon Limited

Printed in U.S.A.

CHAPTER ONE

THE sun was hot, a dazzling colourless disc burning in the incredibly bright blue sky. The faint lulling whisper of the sea somehow calmed Jassy's uneasy mind and the warm stroke of the sunlight relaxed her pale slender limbs as she closed her eyes and languorously stretched out on the smooth warm rocks, giving herself up to the sun and to the blank orange glare behind her eyelids.

She felt tired. It had taken her a good fifteen minutes to swim out to this secluded outcrop of rocks, but she had felt the need to be alone, even though the beach had been almost deserted, and the mechanical, soothing rhythm of all that swimming and the cool sea, sensuously pleasant against her hot skin, had at least taken her mind off her row with Morgan for a while.

A sweet drowsiness crept over her as she sunbathed, her briefly-clad body still cool, as the salt water dried on her skin. A faint scented breeze counteracted the burning heat deceptively and lifted strands of her pale gold hair as she drifted into a light sleep, a slight smile of contentment curving her softly vulnerable mouth, an unconscious grace curving her relaxed young body.

She woke with a start, not knowing how long she had been asleep, but knowing for certain that something had alerted her. She opened her wide brown eyes, blinking in the glare, to find herself looking up into a pair of cool and amused green eyes.

Jassy struggled into a sitting position immediately,

her heart thudding at something in those fierce, mocking eyes, and glanced covertly at the man in front of her wondering how long he had been watching her, embarrassed colour washing over her face at the implications of that thought.

The man had not spoken and Jassy lowered her head, thankful for the heavy curtain of silky golden hair that swung around her face as she did so, hiding her shy embarrassment.

'I'm sorry I had to wake you, beautiful, but you were burning up,' the stranger drawled softly.

Jassy heard the amusement in his cool, low voice and the slight American drawl that gave a deceptive laziness to his words, with confusion and a slight stirring of annoyance and dislike. This man knew he had caught her unawares and he knew that she was embarrassed. He had been watching her sleep for goodness knows how long and she felt invaded, unsettled, that a stranger had been watching her defencelessly sleeping.

He obviously expected some reply, so she lifted her glance to his smooth wide shoulders, finding herself unable to meet those green eyes, and licked her lips nervously.

'I suppose I ought to thank you, then,' she said lightly, managing to inject just the right amount of coolness into her low, clear voice, as she touched the tender red skin on her shoulders that told the truth of his words.

The man smiled, a flash of white teeth in his tanned face, a smile that drew Jassy's breath sharply and involuntarily.

'Go ahead—I won't stop you,' he drawled, mocking her, totally aware of her confusion.

Jassy turned her head away, not bothering to answer him, biting her lip nervously, and wishing he would go away and leave her alone, her wary eyes scanning the hazy blue horizon and resting absently on a tanker that was creeping along the line where the sky met the sea. She felt acutely, deeply aware of the man sitting next to her, disturbed by his presence and the silence seemed to stretch ominously between them until she looked at him again, her wide eyes meeting his with a shock that reverberated throughout her whole body.

'Are . . . are you on holiday here?' she asked in a small nervous voice, needing to talk, and break that silence.

He shook his head, salt water gleaming on his dark hair.

'Business,' he replied shortly, staring at her, his all-seeing gaze sliding down over her soft, rounded, almost naked body in slow appraisal.

Jassy's skin felt hot beneath that hooded gaze and she cursed the impulse that had made her wear the brief violet-coloured bikini that morning. It was far too revealing, as the stranger's dark glance told her, and she longed to cover herself from him.

'Beautiful,' he murmured, smiling faintly as his eyes returned to her very flushed face. 'Quite beautiful.' His voice was a caress and Jassy swallowed convulsively. Without thinking, only knowing that she could not cope with the strange tension that was sparking between them, she slid off the rock into the cool water and began striking out strongly for the beach.

The splash behind her told her that he was following and made her swim faster, her stomach turning over with what she realised was almost fear, coupled with another deeper, trembling emotion that she could not recognise.

It only took him a moment to catch her up and he streaked past her, his brown body cutting through the water with speed and power. Jassy swam on

steadily, irritated, for some reason, with his obvious
show of superiority in the water. So he could swim
better and faster than she could—she had known
that, one look at his powerful, muscular physique
had told her.

It seemed to take forever to reach the shore, and
as she swam with increasingly tired limbs, the dark
man stayed near her, swimming, floating, his
strength making him tireless, his nearness conveying
protection.

At last they reached the beach, with Jassy breathing heavily, hardly able to move her arms and legs
at all, she felt so exhausted. Perhaps it had been a
mistake to swim out so far, and she had not really
considered getting back. Typically me, she thought
wryly as she waded through the shallow water, only
wanting to fling herself on to the hot sand, carefully
not looking at the tall stranger beside her. An instant
later, because she was not paying attention to what
she was doing, her foot caught something sharp
embedded in the sand and she fell, embarrassed and
undignified, splashing into the shallow water with a
small cry of alarm.

The man was beside her immediately, and she felt
the heavy muscles of his arms tightening as they
coiled around her wet body, pulling her to her feet,
then swinging her up against his body.

She pushed at his broad shoulders, her hands
curling in shock against his smooth bare skin as she
found herself pressed to his damp chest a second
later.

'Let me down,' she muttered forcefully, still not
daring to meet his dark and undoubtedly amused
eyes.

He did not answer, but carried her effortlessly up
the deserted beach and deposited her gently on the
soft sand.

Jassy sat perfectly still for a moment, breathing deeply and trying to quell the disturbing confusion that being so near him had aroused, then she pushed back the heavy soaking weight of her hair and looked up at him.

He was standing in front of her, his strong legs planted firmly apart, watching her with lazy green eyes.

'Thank you,' she said quietly, her glance skittering over his hard, lean body. He was very tanned, strong and physically fit, his skin like oiled teak over powerful muscles and sinews. Brief black swimming trunks revealed his hard flat stomach and strong thighs.

Meeting his suddenly intent eyes, Jassy had the strong impression of self-confidence, self-awareness and a certain wildness in him. A free spirit, she thought. Too free.

'Is your foot hurt?' He was still staring, and Jassy felt strangely uneasy as she examined her foot. It was sore, but luckily the skin was not broken.

She shook her golden head. 'No, it will be fine.'

The man smiled. 'Why did you swim out so far?' he asked curiously.

Jassy shrugged, bringing her thoughts back to Morgan. 'I suppose I was running away,' she replied honestly, her voice a little breathless. She got to her feet, feeling out of her depth, still disturbed by his compelling gaze as he watched the graceful movement of her body with veiled eyes.

'At least you're honest, child,' he teased softly.

Jassy's gaze jerked to his face, her brown eyes wide. He had called her 'child', and that rankled, although she probably did look like a schoolgirl, she thought ruefully, with her hair in such disorder and her pale face bare of make-up.

She looked around for her towel and beach-wrap.

She really ought to be getting back to the hotel. Morgan would be wondering where she was.

'I have to go,' she murmured, realising with a shock that her reasons had nothing to do with Morgan, but more with the fact that she did not want this tall stranger thinking of her as a child. 'And thank you again. . . .'

The man frowned slightly. 'I did nothing,' he said firmly. 'But you could do something for me.'

Jassy had lifted her arms and begun wringing out her thick hair, totally unware that such graceful actions drew the man's deep unwavering gaze to her full breasts. She stopped as he spoke, her arms dropping like stones to her sides, a flash of heat searing through her as she caught his expression. Then he smiled again, his lean dark face fiercely attractive, his green eyes warm and persuasive.

'Have dinner with me tonight,' he said softly.

Jassy swallowed, her face flushing. Dinner with this American stranger appealed to her, far too much.

'I'm sorry, I . . . I already have a dinner date,' she stammered, truthfully. She had already promised Morgan and Jassy was disappointed.

The stranger shrugged, his wide shoulders lifting gracefully. 'Some other time, perhaps?' he said gently, as if aware of her fear and nervousness, as if aware that he could frighten her away very easily.

'Yes.' Jassy nodded vaguely. 'I really have to go now. Goodbye.' She turned away from him, not waiting for his reply, and walked over to where she had left her things, aware that he was watching her, every inch of the way.

She glanced round once more as she hurriedly made her way towards the hotel. He had not moved, but was still standing watching her, his powerful body gleaming in the bright light, his dark head

WIPE AWAY THE TEARS

turned towards her, and she did not feel safe until she was out of his view, inside the cool dark reception area of the hotel.

The way he had looked at her had disturbed her more than she realised, awakening a deep unknown response inside her. He had made her aware of him as a devastatingly attractive man, but more than that he had forced her to acknowledge an awareness of herself as a woman, which was a new and strangely exciting experience for her. And she did not even know his name. Shaking her head wretchedly, she frowned as she went up to her room, relieved to be out of range of those clever green eyes.

She showered hurriedly, gasping beneath the cold water, as soon as she reached her room, then dressed in a buttercup-yellow sundress with thin shoulder straps and a low neckline that left her shoulders bare and swung coolly around her slim legs, carefully avoiding the reflection of her slender body in the large mirrors. She brushed out the tousled brightness of her hair and made up her eyes and lips hurriedly, before seeking out Morgan.

She found her stepfather sitting on the balcony of their suite of rooms, reading a Spanish newspaper. He did not hear her barefooted approach, and her eyes lingered affectionately on his long heavy body, somehow incongruously coiled into a delicate-looking cane chair, and shaggy white head bent in concentration, before making her presence known. He could be a monster, but he was the only family Jassy had left, and she loved him.

'Hi, Morgan. Are you going to take me out to lunch?' she asked brightly, dropping a kiss on his white head.

Morgan looked up, his light eyes amused. 'A little early, isn't it?'

Jassy shrugged carelessly, her eyes automatically

skimming the beach below them. She could see no sign of the tall dark stranger.

'I'm starving,' she admitted. 'It must be all this unaccustomed exercise,' she added with a smile.

Morgan folded his newspaper, and got to his feet. 'Perhaps I can persuade Pierre and René to lunch with us,' he remarked blandly, glancing at his watch, his mind obviously scheming.

Jassy spun round to face him with suddenly angry eyes. 'Please don't start that again, Morgan! If you want to lunch with Pierre and René just say so, and I'll make my own arrangements,' she said irritably. Although the earlier row between them—Jassy's reason for escaping to the beach—was forgotten, Morgan had not given up. He made no secret of the fact that he was hoping for Jassy to marry René, and ever since they had arrived on the island he had wasted no time in throwing them together at every opportunity, urging, cajoling and bullying Jassy to be nice to him.

Morgan Carrington was totally and utterly ruthless and cold-blooded when it came to business, using anything and everything to get his own way, even his stepdaughter.

Jassy was well aware of his manipulations, but as they had not yet become too serious, she was trying to put them to the back of her mind. It was not easy.

Morgan smiled now, amused at her irritated outburst, wise enough to know that Jassy was as stubborn as her Mother before her.

'Calm down, Jassy,' he said placatingly, taking her arm. 'We'll lunch together, just the two of us. I didn't mean to upset you.'

Jassy smiled, aware of his cunning, but her irritation was forgotten. 'Shall we eat here, or in town?'

'It's up to you, darling, which would you prefer?'

Jassy knew that he was trying to get round her.

'In town,' she decided, after considering for a moment.

They took the lift downstairs and strolled out to Morgan's car, still arm in arm. The air was still and terribly hot and Jassy could feel the heat of the concrete pavement through her thin sandals. Beautiful weather, she thought happily, lifting her face to the sun.

The roof was down on the expensive sports car that Morgan had hired for their stay here, and as the car picked up speed along the coast road, the blissfully cool breeze whipped Jassy's long hair around her face as she stared dreamily at the sparkling blue sea.

They lunched under rainbow parasols in a streetside café picked out by Jassy, both choosing fish, a local speciality, and salad. Morgan was unusually quiet.

'What's worrying you, Morgan?' Jassy finally asked, after chatting to virtually no response for most of the meal. She twirled her wine glass nervously, feeling vaguely uneasy as she stared at him, waiting for his answer. Perhaps he and Pierre had run into difficulties with the land deal—their reason for being on the island—they were currently involved in. Jassy had seen the plans for the huge hotel and pleasure complex, lying around in the suite, but had not paid much attention.

Morgan frowned, his almost colourless eyes meeting hers briefly before veering away.

'Nothing for you to worry about, my darling,' he answered evasively. 'Business.'

Jassy sighed. It was always business. The man she had met on the beach had come to the island on business, she remembered. At the thought of him her mind became crowded with his image, his hard brown body, his mocking and intent green eyes, his lazy American voice. He did not have the look of a businessman, the jaded cunning that she had seen so often in Morgan and his associates. He looked free and wild, and it surprised her to realise that she remembered every single second of her brief and embarrassing encounter with him. He was lingering in her mind in a way no other casual acquaintance had before. It was extremely disturbing.

Morgan was still silent and preoccupied as they finished lunch and Jassy decided to leave him to it, knowing from bitter experience that when her step-father's mind was on business, there was nothing she could do to gain his attention.

'I think I'll do some shopping while we're here in town, care to come with me?' She knew what his answer would be before he shook his head. So promising to take a taxi back to the hotel, and refusing the crisp wad of notes he tried to press into her hands, she picked up her straw shoulder bag and left the café.

She calculated that she had a couple of hours before most of the shops closed for the afternoon siesta, and she planned to make the most of them. She strolled slowly down the bright, dusty streets, ignoring the blatant remarks of young, dark-skinned men who did not hide their appreciation of her un-usual fair beauty, exploring leisurely the small dark shops that were literally crammed with fine examples of local crafts. Being an only child, she was used to doing things alone, and her cool independence rendered her more than capable of fending off ardent admirers, as she made her purchases.

She bought a beautiful terracotta vase for Beth, Morgan's long-suffering housekeeper, cheerfully bargaining with the stout, smiling shopkeeper, and then wandered into the nearby bazaar, fascinated by the noise and the warm mixture of smells that issued from the densely-packed stalls. She bought a silver tie-pin for Morgan and some filigree earrings for her best friend Lavender, and then dithered over a silver bracelet for herself, finally deciding to leave it for the moment.

As she emerged from the bazaar the sunlight hit her forcefully and she began to wish that she had brought a hat with her, unused as she was to such relentless heat. She blinked in the blinding glare for a few seconds, deciding that her throat was so parched it was time for a long cool drink and an opportunity to sit down for a while.

She stood on the edge of the pavement awaiting her chance to dodge through the fast-moving stream of traffic to a café on the other side of the road, when a low red sports car pulled up in front of her. Ready to rebuff any advances from its driver, Jassy found herself staring at René Moreau, whose blue eyes were shining with amusement at her cold face.

'Hello, Jassy. All ready to give me the cold shoulder, eh?' His English was perfect and he laughed as he spoke.

Jassy found herself smiling back. 'You foreign men, you're all the same,' she teased.

René shrugged, characteristically French. 'You're a beautiful girl, what can you expect?' His eyes slid over her openly.

Jassy raised her eyebrows, not in the least insulted by his behaviour, obvious though it was. René was young and she had known him long enough not to take him seriously.

'Do you want a lift, or are you still shopping?'

'Actually, I'm trying to make my way across the road to that café,' Jassy admitted, pointing in front of her. 'Without much success. Everyone drives like a madman here!'

René laughed again and leaning over, swung open the door of his car.

'Get in and come for a drink with me,' he said persuasively.

Jassy hesitated for a second, then slid in beside him. She felt too hot and thirsty to argue.

Putting his foot on the accelerator, René shot the low car into the stream of traffic again, ignoring the loud blaring of horns that accompanied his actions. Jassy shut her eyes, not wanting to look, because René's driving was reckless in the extreme and he did not appreciate words of caution.

She did not open her eyes until the car screeched to a halt outside an expensive-looking restaurant. Letting out a long sigh of relief, she stumbled out of the car, glad to have her feet on the ground again, watching René jumping out over his door rather than opening it. He strolled round to her, whistling softly as he removed his sunglasses, and took her arm.

'Have you had lunch?' Not giving her time to answer, he continued, 'I haven't and I'm famished. This place is highly recommended.'

They entered the restaurant and sat down. René ordered a huge meal and tried to persuade Jassy to have something to eat. She refused, ordering a glass of freshly-made, iced lemonade.

'A dirty trick,' she said without reproach as she sipped her cold drink gratefully, a few moments later. René looked up innocently, and Jassy laughed. 'You know what I'm talking about.'

He smiled, 'How else could I persuade you to have lunch with me?' he asked simply.

'You couldn't—I've already had lunch,' she replied.

'Precisely.' René returned his attention to the shellfish in front of him, without remorse, and Jassy gave up. It did not matter, and at least her thirst was quenched, and the restaurant was cool, beautifully cool. She slipped off her sandals under the table and rested her hot and aching feet on the blissfully cold marble floor, watching René as he ate.

She had known him for just over a year, having first met him when Morgan invited Pierre—René's father—to dinner at their house in London. Pierre Moreau was a wealthy French industrialist and at the time Morgan had been anxious to set up a deal with him.

Pierre had brought René with him that evening and the two young people had been left to their own devices as soon as dinner was over, when Morgan and Pierre had disappeared into Morgan's impressive study to talk business. René was young and arrogant, but he could also be charming and, on occasions, kind. Pierre was hand-grooming him to take over his vast and wealthy industrial empire, so that he could retire, and Jassy had been amazed at René's fatalistic acceptance of this situation. He did not seem particularly interested in his father's business, in fact, pretty girls and fast cars seemed to be infinitely more important to him. Jassy had immediately recognised the similarity of their lives.

Both, although to a lesser extent in Jassy's case, were overshadowed and manipulated by powerful, wealthy fathers and would have their lives channelled and organised by these ruthless, ambitious men, whom they loved too much to really doubt.

The only difference between Jassy and René was that René would accept without demur, while Jassy felt, with dread, that she would have to fight Morgan in the end. This difference however was slight, easily outweighed by the similarity, and a wary friendship had sprung up between them almost immediately.

There had never been any romance between them, though. Jassy had made sure of that, gently freezing René's easy sexual advances, but the bond was fairly strong—they understood everything about each other's lives.

They had met a number of times since that first dinner, in many places around the world, always with their respective fathers, and Jassy was always pleased to see him, glad of his amusing and undemanding company.

She brought her mind back to the present and studied René objectively. He was very attractive, she supposed, although he did not affect her at all, never making her heart beat faster. He had light brown hair and an olive complexion, confident blue eyes and a slim, graceful body. Great self-assurance cloaked him and he seemed, to Jassy's inexperienced eyes, to be very French, somehow.

He caught her looking at him and smiled. 'You are very pensive, Jassy,' he said softly.

She sighed. 'Are you happy, René?' she asked candidly, feeling suddenly and absurdly worried about him.

'Happy? Of course I'm happy. I have a full stomach, a glass of excellent wine, and a beautiful luncheon companion. What more could I ask?' he replied, flippantly, not appearing at all surprised by her question, as he lit a strong-smelling French cigarette with thin careless hands.

'I'm talking about the business. Do you really want to take over from Pierre?' she questioned seriously.

The laughter died in René's eyes.

'What I want is not so important. I have always known what was in store for me; as you have. Papa will retire in a year or two, and in a way—yes, I want to take over. Power is very attractive, you know, Jassy, especially when you have been bred for it,' he said seriously.

Jassy considered his confident answer and saw for the first time a certain hardness in him. Perhaps he was more like Pierre than she had realised. Perhaps it was only his youth that had deceived her into thinking that he was like her. She was holding back from committing herself to what Morgan wanted for her, but René was ready and obviously willing to be what Pierre wanted him to be.

'Morgan is hoping that you and I will marry,' she said worriedly, voicing her fears.

'Would it be such a bad idea?' René asked softly, his eyes still serious.

Jassy stared at him in amazement, unable to tell if he were joking or not, but not wanting to find out.

'Can I have another lemonade, please?' she asked huskily, lowering her eyes in confusion. René laughed out loud and beckoned the attentive waiter. After ordering her lemonade, he turned back to her and watched her with amused and unusually-hard eyes.

'Don't be afraid, *chérie*,' he said carelessly. 'You think I'm ganging up with Morgan against you, yes?'

Jassy glared at him; he could be so infuriating! She wished he would change the subject.

'I certainly wouldn't put it past Morgan, I don't know about you, although I'm beginning to wonder,' she retorted drily, feeling suddenly out of her depth, as if René was a stranger, not the carefree young man she knew. She sipped her lemonade quickly.

'Perhaps that is why you are afraid,' René said quietly. 'You don't know me very well at all, do you Jassy?'

She lifted her clear brown eyes to his. 'Don't play games with me, René,' she said steadily. 'It's far too hot!' And time to leave, she decided. She picked up her bag. 'Thanks for the lemonade,' she smiled as she got to her feet.

'I'll drive you back to your hotel,' René offered smoothly, counting notes from his pocket.

Jassy swung her heavy hair impatiently over her shoulder. 'I'll get a taxi,' she argued, not at all sure that she wanted any more of René's company at the moment.

'I'll drive you,' he repeated, his mouth tightening slightly. 'I have to see Morgan anyway.'

'About what?' Jassy asked curiously. Had René been speaking the truth? Did he intend to join forces with Morgan against her? She shook her head angrily. She was getting paranoid about the whole business. She would have to pull herself together! René merely smiled as he took her arm.

'Mind your own business,' he said lightly, as they stepped out of the restaurant and into the fierce early afternoon sun.

The town was much quieter, most of its inhabitants sleeping, as René made his way to the coast road. Lost in her own thoughts, Jassy did not pay much attention to his reckless driving.

They stopped at a red traffic light and as René drummed his fingers impatiently on the steering wheel, Jassy glanced round idly, her eyes suddenly riveting on the tall, powerful and familiar figure of a man, sliding gracefully out of a black Mercedes on the other side of the road. Her breath seemed to stick in her throat as she watched him, recognising him as the stranger from the beach that morning. She was amazed at her trembling reaction to the sight of him, lean and almost painfully attractive in a light, expensively cut suit, as he strolled indolently around the front of the car and opened the passenger door.

Jassy stared at him openely. He looked strong and

sophisticated, different from the man who had gently taunted her on the beach, his vital black hair neat, his brown muscular body hidden beneath tailored cloth.

The traffic lights were changing and Jassy only glimpsed the woman who got out of the black Mercedes—tall and stylishly slender in a dusky pink dress, with a cloud of raven-black hair, she took the stranger's arm with a familiarity that Jassy recognised with a sinking heart as intimacy.

Then René's car had swung around the corner and the couple were lost from view.

'What were you looking at?' René asked lazily, taking his eyes off the road for a second.

'I thought I recognised somebody,' Jassy replied half-truthfully, not wanting to talk to René about the dark stranger, but knowing that she had caught his quick attention and excited his curiosity by the craning of her neck.

'Shall I switch the radio on?' she asked brightly.

René nodded brusquely, a little put out at her deliberate evasion, his mouth a trifle sullen.

The rest of their journey back to Jassy's hotel passed in silence. She had turned the radio on loud, although she was not listening to it, she was thinking about the man from the beach, wondering at her fierce reaction to him, wondering about the beautiful woman who had been in his car. Were they lovers? Were they married? She felt a strange and instant dislike for that lovely, unknown woman, and with a shock that stopped her breath for a moment, the realisation hit her that she was jealous. She shook her golden head dazedly—it really was too ridiculous. She did not know him at all, certainly not enough to feel that she had any claim on him. Why couldn't she put him out of her mind?

The car skidded to a noisy halt, physically jerking

Jassy out of her reverie, and she looked up to find herself at the hotel entrance. René snapped off the radio, flashing her a dark look, and they got out of the car.

Reaching the suite, she turned to him and smiled. 'Thanks for the lift.'

He kissed both her cheeks affectionately. 'The pleasure was mine,' he said gallantly, his earlier moodiness disappearing. He did not move and Jassy remembered suddenly that he was here for a purpose. She giggled. 'I forgot, you've come to see Morgan,' she apologised, throwing open the ornate doors.

Her stepfather was working at his huge desk in the lounge and lifted his shaggy head with a smile of satisfaction when he saw Jassy and René together.

'René, good to see you, my boy!' he said heartily, getting to his feet and shaking the younger man's hand.

'René gave me a lift back from the town,' Jassy explained, kissing her stepfather's cheek. 'And if you two are going to talk business, I think I'll go for a nap before dinner.' She was hot and sticky and very tired, and if, as she suspected, Morgan and René were going to talk about her and the possibility of a forthcoming marriage, she did not want to know, not at the moment anyway.

She strolled into her bedroom still wondering at the hard emotion she had seen in René's eyes at the restaurant, and closed her eyes trying to dislodge these thoughts. She was probably overreacting. Of late, she had been feeling more and more trapped, as if Morgan was finally moving in for the kill—a suitable cliché, she thought bitterly. But however much he bullied and manipulated she would not marry René.

I won't even think about it, she told herself

fiercely. There's no use worrying until I know for sure what Morgan's plans are. She stripped off her yellow sundress and strolled into the sumptuous private bathroom that adjoined her bedroom, to take a cold shower, carefully blanking out her mind to everything but the pelting refreshing coldness of the water on her dusty overheated body.

Dressed in a thin cotton wrap, five minutes later, she pulled closed the slatted wooden blinds on her bedroom windows, and lay down on her bed, in the dim artificially-cool room, falling almost immediately into a light uneasy sleep.

CHAPTER TWO

'Jassy, wake up, it's after seven!' Morgan shook her shoulder gently, an indulgent smile curving his lips, as Jassy forced open her eyes.

'It's after seven,' he repeated patiently.

'After seven? Oh, God!' She sat up abruptly, wondering how she could have possibly slept for so long.

'You must have needed the rest,' her stepfather said, answering her unspoken question.

He was already dressed for dinner, his dark evening suit lending him an air of quiet dignity.

'I would have woken you earlier, but René only left fifteen minutes ago.'

It was on the tip of Jassy's tongue to ask what they had found to talk about for over four hours, but she restrained herself. There was no point in asking for trouble, and given the slightest hint of encouragement Morgan would not hesitate to press his case.

'I'll get ready,' was all she said as she swung her legs off the bed. Morgan smiled at her obedience.

'There's no rush,' he rejoined lightly. 'I've invited Pierre and René for dinner,'

Who else? Jassy thought wryly.

'And also Max Bellmer. He flew in yesterday. Apparently his sister lives here—she married a Spaniard who owns a string of hotels, including this one, I believe,' Morgan continued, sounding well pleased with himself, but Jassy was not paying much attention.

One businessman was much the same as another to her. Morgan left her room in search of a drink, and after washing, she applied her make-up carefully, absently examining herself in the mirror.

She was a tall girl with a slender curved body. Thick, straight blonde hair hung over her shoulders and her face was quite beautiful, the bone structure delicate, her skin pale and flawless.

Her wide brown eyes were innocent, shy and intelligent, her nose small and straight, and her mouth gently curved and vulnerable. She was aware of her beauty without conceit, never paying much attention to it, and often finding it more of a drawback than an asset. This, coupled with the fact that long familiarity with her looks gave her plenty to criticise—she had always thought that her mouth was too large—had long since stripped her of any vanity, leaving her often unaware of her potent attraction to the opposite sex.

She was naturally quiet and sensitive, her shyness veiling a charming wit and depth of character, often hidden by her cool, remote manner. But one look into her clear eyes revealed her inner warmth, and her amusing perceptive intelligence. Her wary outer shell had been carefully constructed for the life she lived with Morgan.

She brushed out her pale hair, leaving it loose to fall soft and silky against her bare shoulders, then stepped into the black dress she had chosen for dinner, a tight sheath that clung sensuously to her lissom figure, with a tight, low bodice held up by slender straps that left her arms and shoulders bare. It was a daring, deliberately seductive dress, chosen by Morgan on a shopping trip in Paris.

When she left her boarding school and went to live with him in London, Jassy had had little idea of the life she would have to lead. Neither had she realised the full extent of her stepfather's entertaining. He had made it clear that he found most of her clothes unsuitable and had whisked her off to Paris, where they had spent a full week refurbishing her wardrobe with a number of daring and exotic evening dresses, of which the black dress she wore tonight was one.

Jassy had protested at first, hardly recognising the beautiful, alluring woman who stared back at her from the mirror when she wore these dresses. But Morgan had been very persuasive—he wanted to be proud of her, both he and his associates appreciated a beautiful woman at the dinner table, he had told her—and she had finally given in to him. It made him happy, and she owed him a lot, and it did not really matter to her what she wore in the evenings. The dresses were, after all, very lovely even if they did not accurately reflect her character.

Pouting at herself in the mirror, Jassy stepped into high-heeled black sandals, and glancing at the clock on the dressing-table saw that it was just after eight, time to join Morgan.

She found her stepfather out on the huge balcony with Pierre and René, who had already arrived. Pierre kissed her hand gallantly, commenting on her beauty, and René kissed both her cheeks, adding his own extravagant compliments on her appearance, while Morgan fetched her a drink. His pride was shining in his light eyes as he handed her a small whisky and soda, and smiling at him, Jassy was suddenly glad that she could please him so easily.

They all sat down in the ornate chairs on the balcony, the men chatting and Jassy let her gaze wander towards the dark, shifting sea. The night was warm and balmy, the powerful scent from the garden below, sweetening the warm air, and frail insects hummed loudly, almost to the beat of the faintly pounding ocean.

Jassy would have been content to sit there all

night, her eyes full of dreams, her ears full of muted evening noises. Indeed, so lost was she in her own thoughts that she did not notice Morgan getting to his feet to welcome his third guest, only turning her head when she heard herself being introduced, a polite smile curving her gentle mouth as Morgan said, 'Max, my daughter Jassy.'

She lifted her eyes and found herself staring into a pair of veiled and amused green ones.

It was the man from the beach, the dark American stranger, and for a second her heart stopped beating altogether, and then began to thump slowly and painfully as she dragged her gaze from the compelling brilliance of his.

Max Bellmer took her hand in his and drew it to his hard mouth, brushing her knuckles briefly with his warm lips. Jassy quivered, his touch tingling fire that shot through her whole body. 'Miss Carrington and I have already met,' he drawled softly, his low voice sending shivers down her spine.

'Really?' Morgan's eyes sharpened with interest. 'That's quite a coincidence. Where?'

Max Bellmer smiled, his eyes strangely gentle as they rested on Jassy's flushed face.

'At the beach, this morning,' he replied, not revealing any of the details, for which Jassy was thankful. She withdrew her hand from his, trying to ignore the flash of amusement in his green eyes at her nervous, obvious gesture, and lowered her head. Morgan was still watching them both, a speculative gleam in his eyes, and Jassy had to bite her lip to stop herself from smiling. She could almost hear Morgan's scheming mind ticking over as he assessed the possibilities of this new situation.

For herself, she felt intensely shocked by Max Bellmer's appearance, and was profoundly relieved to hear Morgan diverting his attention and his probing green eyes by offering him a drink. Pierre was asking polite questions, and within the next five minutes Max Bellmer was drawn into light conversation with the two older men, leaving Jassy to watch him surreptitiously from beneath her lashes.

She had been thinking about him all day, wondering if she would see him again, and now he was going to have dinner with them. It was like magic, and she felt happy.

He wore a superbly-tailored white dinner jacket that could not conceal the power and strength of his body, its light colour contrasting vividly with his tanned skin and thick dark hair. She watched his face as he talked. It was hard-boned and lean, with stark cheekbones and a strong jaw. The green eyes glittered with knowledge and amusement, from beneath heavy lids, and his mouth was beautifully moulded, hard, warm and sensual.

He was the most fascinating and attractive man Jassy had ever seen, and she stared and stared, unable to take her eyes off him.

As if aware of her close scrutiny, he suddenly turned his head towards her and their eyes met, locking fiercely, before Jassy could lower her head. His hard mouth softened into a smile as he held her wide, innocent gaze, and she felt a sweet and tense excitement rising inside her at the warm charm of that smile.

They stared at each other for what seemed to Jassy like years, then René was beside her, slipping his arm possessively around her slim bare shoulders, and in the second before they broke eye contact, Jassy saw Max Bellmer's dark brows draw together frowningly at René's casual, intimate action.

She turned from him then, unable to bear the censure she imagined she saw in his eyes, and smiled at René. He had seen her staring at Max Bellmer and his young mouth was faintly sullen.

'You find him attractive, yes?' he asked her flatly, making it more of a statement than a question.

'What is the matter with you, René?' Jassy asked with surprise, deliberately not answering his question.

René sighed, trying to look repentant. 'Forgive me. I think I'm jealous,' he said grandly.

Jassy snorted with disbelief. 'And I think you're mad,' she replied mildly, realising now why he had put his arm around her shoulders so possessively.

René shrugged. 'Ever since he arrived you've been watching him,' he complained peevishly.

Had she been that obvious? Jassy wondered. Even if she had, it was nothing to do with René.

'What were you talking to Morgan about, this afternoon?' she questioned, changing the subject.

'Many things,' René replied evasively, still sounding annoyed, and in consequence rather spiteful. 'You were right, Morgan does want us to be married.'

'He actually said that?' Jassy was amazed and could not hide it.

'I think it is a good idea,' René stated arrogantly.

Jassy pushed his arm from her shoulders and stared at him in utter disbelief. 'You can't be serious!' she whispered, unable to keep the horror out of her voice.

René stiffened, his mouth pursing. 'I do not joke about marriage,' he snapped angrily.

Before Jassy could reply, dinner was announced and their conversation interrupted. Profoundly relieved, she went indoors and they all sat down around the beautifully laid table, sparkling with crystal and silver.

Jassy was shaken by what René had said. They had joked about the idea of getting married the last time they met in New York; it had never been anything serious between them. Never! Since they had been on the island, however, René's attitude had changed and he really did seem too serious about the whole business. She flashed Morgan an irritated glance, wondering, not unfairly, what incentive he had offered René. The time was coming for their biggest confrontation, and Jassy was not looking forward to it.

Lifting her head, she found Max Bellmer staring at her across the table with inscrutable, intent eyes. Her inner turmoil was obvious in her clouded eyes, creased forehead and the defeated bow of her slender neck. Suddenly there was a deeply perceptive quality in his expression that seemed to touch something raw and painful inside her; as though he could find out anything and everything about her, just by assessing her with his clever green eyes. Then it was gone and he was smiling at her, making all her worries disappear under the magnetic force of his personality.

'Fate,' he said, very softly so that only she could hear, raising his glass to hers.

Jassy knew what he meant, and soft, becoming colour flooded her small face.

'You knew?' she asked with a gentle smile, her eyes on his strong brown hand curled lazily round the fragile crystal glass.

'The moment I saw you,' he teased in his low American voice.

And whether or not it was true, Jassy could well believe that he did know. The sweet, dizzying excitement was still churning inside her as she looked into his lean dark face.

'You look very lovely tonight,' Max said deeply, and Jassy shivered.

'Thank you,' she whispered, feeling well and truly out of her depth with him, lowering her shining head and trying to concentrate on the tempting, delicious food in front of her.

Morgan was talking to Max then, and Jassy's attention, most of it anyway, was captured by Pierre who was seated by her side, and the meal passed enjoyably with no further direct contact between Jassy and Max.

She did not talk much, not only because she was naturally shy, but also because Morgan did not encourage it on occasions like this. He had told her that 'bright, overpowering, chattering women' could not be tolerated at his dinner table. As long as they looked good, that was all that was needed. When he had given her these instructions Jassy had laughed, but she had also felt hurt. He might as well have tailors' dummies at his table, she had thought. But now she obeyed, satisfied to listen to the others with vague attention.

Tonight she was sensitively aware of every movement Max Bellmer made, every smile, every turn of his proud dark head, every shifting of his powerful body. She also listened carefully to every word he said, familiarising herself with that low, drawling voice that affected her senses so violently.

With dinner finished, they were served with coffee and brandy by the silent waiters and the men lit cigars, the rough fragrance spiralling around the cool room. Jassy sipped her brandy with slow pleasure, accepting a cigarette from René and listening to the deep, lazy laughter of Max Bellmer.

It was one of her favourite times of the day, late evening, when everybody was relaxed and satisfied, and when laughter came easily. She was aware of Max Bellmer's eyes upon her again, hooded, unreadable and faintly brooding, and raised her head to hear Morgan saying jovially, 'But René practically *is* my son, Pierre, my old friend. There's only the formalities now.'

Jassy's eyes widened with pure shock as she looked at her stepfather. How could Morgan be so unsubtle, so tactless? she wondered miserably, fighting her strong urge to run from the room.

She would not marry René—not even for Morgan, she thought bitterly, gathering her composure with difficulty so that when her eyes next met those of Max Bellmer, she could meet his brooding stare with calm dignity, her humiliation and embarrassment at Morgan's careless words well hidden.

The evening passed quickly, but as Jassy sat on her bed several hours later, she knew that she would not sleep. She felt too confused and upset by what Morgan had said. He had pushed her towards René in the past, that was true, but he had never been so obvious or so public about it before. Perhaps he felt confident now that he had René on his side, although Jassy was finding René's attitude just as difficult to understand. As far as she was concerned, they were just friends and she could not, would not believe that René loved her. Which meant that there must be some ulterior motive behind his willingness to marry her, some privately arranged business deal between Morgan and Pierre.

She lowered her head into her shaking hands, feeling physically sick. She would not let herself be manipulated by Morgan as though she were a piece of property! Everything inside her cried out against it. She would talk to him in the morning. It would not be easy, but her fear of being used, a strong, deep-rooted fear, would help her to fight him and please God, let me win, she prayed.

Her thoughts turned to Max Bellmer, and her chaotic feelings for him. She hardly knew him and yet she was deeply attracted to him in every way.

She had learned over dinner that he was a wealthy merchant banker. His wealth and power had been obvious to her before she learned of his profession, not only because she could tell it just by looking at him, but because she had seen the respect and fear in Morgan's eyes, his obvious need to impress.

Jassy jumped restlessly to her feet and looked out of the window. It was a warm and beautiful night, the sky pitch-black, scattered with tiny stars, and lit by an almost full moon. It seemed to call to her, the bedroom becoming unbearably claustrophobic. She would go for a swim and forget her troubles.

She struggled out of her tight black dress and slipped on a bikini, covering it with a short loose caftan, then ran barefoot from her room and down to the beach.

The vast expanse of pale sand was empty, totally deserted, and silky beneath her toes. Even though she knew it was an illusion, she suddenly felt free and bursting with the pure happiness of being alive.

She pulled the caftan off over her head and began to dance, remembering all the ballet lessons she had taken at school, humming to herself as she gracefully pirouetted her slender body, a pale blur in the darkness. It was a night to do crazy, happy things, and she laughed aloud as she ran into the warm, silver-scattered sea, swimming, diving and floating until she felt deliciously tired.

She waded out of the water then, still singing to herself, only to stop stock-still, her heart pounding heavily as she fearfully surveyed the tall menacing figure of a man a few yards in front of her, blocking her pathway up the beach.

'Jassy.' He spoke her name softly, the noise coming from deep within his throat, and she breathed a shaken sigh of relief mingled with the same sweet excitement she had felt before.

'Mr Bellmer, you frightened me,' she murmured, with a nervous little laugh, walking towards him. He stood perfectly still, watching her with dark, hooded eyes as she approached, watching the moonlight rippling on her smooth, pale body, watching her nervousness.

And Jassy watched him too, from beneath her lashes, her eyes almost hungry. He was barefooted, his dinner-jacket gone, his shirt open low at his tanned throat. She stood before him, smoothing back the pale silk of her hair with nervous hands.

He smiled. 'You're out late.' He was deliberately casual, putting her at ease.

Jassy laughed gently. 'I couldn't stay in my room, I felt trapped, so I thought I'd come for a swim. I didn't realise until I got here how beautiful it is tonight.' She looked up into his hard, still face. 'Do you know what I mean?'

Max Bellmer sighed heavily, staring down at the pure lines of her upturned face.

'Yes, I know what you mean,' he said softly. His glance lifted towards the horizon, remote and unreadable, to Jassy's eager eyes.

'I watched you dancing,' he said expressionlessly.

'Oh!' She was lost for words, wondering if she had made a fool of herself. 'How embarrassing,' she whispered, and turned away from him, wondering where she had left her caftan.

She shivered uncontrollably as he placed his hands gently on her bare shoulders and propelled her round to face him again, the touch of his strong fingers heating the damp skin they touched.

'Never embarrassing, Jassy. You were beautiful, truly beautiful.' His voice was slightly harsh.

'Mr Bellmer——'

'Max. Come on, say it, it's not so very difficult,' he teased, his green eyes amused.

'Max.' She tried saying it and it sounded good. 'You're right, it's not difficult at all,' she agreed flippantly, smiling at him.

His hands were still resting lightly on her shoulders and Jassy was acutely aware of his touch. Her heart was beating painfully fast at such intimate contact, and fearing that he would hear it and guess how she was feeling, she moved back abruptly and he released her. She immediately regretted her move, and feeling that everything was going wrong somehow, she sighed miserably.

'I'm going in now,' she said quietly, feeling unaccountably depressed. Max watched the sadness clouding her eyes.

'Stay and talk to me instead,' he suggested persuasively.

Jassy flashed him a radiant smile. He wanted her to stay with him for a while longer! She had felt sure that he was bored with her, and that had prompted her suggested retreat. Now she was happy again.

'Did you come out for a walk?' she asked shyly, her eyes bright.

'Perhaps I was waiting for you,' he replied, sounding quite serious, his eyes never leaving her face.

'You didn't know I was coming out for a swim, did you?'

He caught her pointed chin in hard-skinned fingers and tilted it upwards, so that the moonlight caught her pale face and unshadowed her eyes.

'Maybe not. But I do know that you were unhappy at dinner tonight, desperately unhappy,' he said gently.

The concern in his low voice loosened the careful shell that Jassy had constructed around her problems, leaving her painfully vulnerable, and she could not control the swift tears that flooded into her eyes.

She could not hide them either, because Max still held her face gently but firmly, turning those damnable tears to liquid silver spilling down her face.

He swore softly and violently under his breath, and a second later he pulled her into the strong circle of his arms, bending her golden head to his shoulder, holding her tightly. The last frail shreds of her careful control dissolved with his nearness, with his smooth hard shoulder beneath her cheek, with the clean warm smell of him filling her nostrils, and her tears flooded forth, shaking her body and soaking his shirt as she clung to him, sobbing uncontrollably for long releasing minutes.

'Jassy, Jassy.' He groaned her name softly, his fingers threading through her wet hair and pushing it back gently from her face in a rhythmic, soothing motion.

Jassy cried until her tears dried up, the release strengthening her as she finally quietened. Max continued to hold her until she lifted her damp face and managed to smile shakily up at him. He released her then, leaving her with a strong sense of loneliness, and produced some cigarettes from his trouser pocket.

'Do you want one?'

Jassy nodded and he placed one between her lips with a smile, the moonlight catching on his dark hair as he bent to light it for her. She drew on it strongly, her trusting eyes never leaving his lean face.

'Your shirt . . . I'm sorry,' she whispered huskily, needing to excuse her behaviour and apologise. Max shrugged gracefully, exhaling smoke in a long thin stream.

'Forget it,' he replied, sounding as though he meant it, his green eyes narrowed in careful scrutiny on her face.

Jassy lowered her head, very glad that he could not see the colour flooding her cheeks. There was something strangely intimate about crying in a stranger's arms on a deserted moonlit beach. She felt that she had given away some part of herself that she always kept hidden, and it worried her a little.

'Shall we walk?' The deep, cool voice made her start. He was holding out his hand to her.

'I'd like to find my caftan first,' she said breathlessly, hesitating very slightly before letting her small hand become encased in his larger one.

He scanned the beach and pointed. 'Over there.'

They strolled in that direction and he watched her as she slipped it over her head, and her skin felt heated as she glanced up and saw the expression in his eyes. The caftan reached to mid-thigh, leaving her long slim legs bare, but at least it was respectable.

'Very fetching,' Max drawled lazily, reading her mind.

Jassy smiled as he took her hand again, glancing covertly at his strong, clear profile as they walked. His mood was very different from that at dinner, and different again from their first meeting. He seemed quiet and sympathetic, thoughtful and perhaps a little distant—obviously he was a man of many sides.

He turned his head suddenly and caught her watching him. His beautifully-moulded mouth curved into a faint smile.

'Want to talk about it?'

'I feel embarrassed . . . for crying the way I did,' she murmured haltingly, turning away towards the glinting sea.

'There's no need. I don't find it at all embarrassing—everybody needs a shoulder to cry on sometimes,' Max replied lightly, flicking her hair teasingly.

And whose shoulder do you cry on? Jassy wondered silently. The beautiful woman she had seen stepping out of his Mercedes? The thought pained her.

'Thank you for being so understanding,' was all she said in answer, her voice low and defensive.

Max stopped walking abruptly, pulling her round to face him.

'Dear God, Jassy, is there no getting through to you?' he asked irritably. 'How long do you think you can bottle these things up inside yourself?'

His steel-strong fingers were digging into her fragile shoulders, bruising her, and jealous thoughts of the woman who had been in his car made her ungracious in reply.

'Why should you care?' she demanded defiantly.

Max sighed, his mouth twisting. 'Why indeed?' he asked flatly, raking her stubborn face with cool eyes.

Jassy stared into the harsh lines of his face and did not want him to be annoyed with her. What he said was true. She did need somebody to confide in, and with a shock of realisation she knew that she trusted this powerful American, without knowing why. He was so very different from any man she had ever met before.

'It's Morgan,' she blurted out suddenly. Max's fingers eased their pressure on her shoulders.

'Your father? I guessed as much.'

'He's not my father, I never knew my real father. Morgan is my stepfather,' she explained in an expressionless voice.

'And your mother?' Max probed gently.

Jassy swallowed. 'My mother died when I was twelve. She had a terminal illness,' she said huskily. Max drew breath slowly, shaking his dark head in disbelief.

'I'm sorry, Jassy,' he said quietly.

She managed a weak smile. 'Don't be sorry for me,' she returned steadily, not wanting his pity.

'Tell me about it.' Max's voice was gentle and persuasive.

They stood facing each other on the pale sand, only inches between them, not touching each other but looking into each other's faces openly and without deceit.

Jassy shrugged nervously, wondering where to start.

'My father was killed in an accident at his factory just before I was born. I never even saw him . . . but my mother had some photos of him. Morgan didn't want her to keep them, so she gave them to me. . . . I still hide them from him.' She paused, her eyes firmly on her bare toes, clenching in the powdery sand. 'Five years later my mother married Morgan. He swept her off her feet, I think, she was very lonely . . . and he can be very charming, and he pursues what he wants ruthlessly.

'I think they loved each other, especially at the beginning, although he never put her before the business——' Jassy broke off, aware of how bitter she sounded. Morgan had never let his wife intrude on the most important part of his life. Business was business, he always said, as though that were a good excuse.

Jassy was sure that her mother had been under no illusions as to the first love of Morgan's life, but perhaps she had never expected to be cut out of his life so completely. Morgan had wanted a son to carry on the business, but when it had become clear that Jassy's mother could not bear him that son, he had turned away from her like a spiteful child, behaving with indifference towards her, trying to get back at her for what he considered the injury done to him, for her shortcomings.

Jassy was also aware that Morgan wished that she was a man, although, making the best of a bad job, he was determined that she should marry well. If he did not have a son of his own, then he was making sure that he handpicked a son-in-law and that was what Jassy could not take.

She was aware that Morgan had some affection for her, but knew that it would not stop him making use of her. People did not exist to her stepfather, except in terms of what they could do for him. His obsession was business and Jassy saw the coldness in him—and the weakness.

The weakness displayed itself in his gambling. Morgan was so used to winning, to getting his own way that gambling was a fascinating challenge to him. He could lose thousands of pounds in one night and not turn a hair.

Jassy knew that at this very moment he would be in the hotel casino. She sighed. It did not really make any difference what Morgan was; the fact still remained that he was the nearest thing to a family that she had, and despite everything, she did love him.

'It's natural that you care for him,' Max said quietly, reading her mind, carefully watching the conflict of emotions chasing across her pointed face. 'But he's weak, Jassy, you must see that.'

Jassy nodded, knowing that Max was trying to help her.

'I do care for him, but I'm not blind to his faults,' she whispered ruefully.

'And René Moreau?' Max's catlike eyes were intent, his long body still, as though he had been waiting to ask this question for a long, long time.

Jassy ran her fingers through her hair, anxiety in her brown eyes. 'Morgan wants me to marry him.' Her voice broke as she admitted out loud what had been troubling her so.

'And you?' he persisted relentlessly, a flicker of unrecognisable emotion darkening his lean face.

'I don't want to marry René, and I know that I can't let Morgan use me the way he used my mother. That's why I couldn't sleep tonight—I know that the time is coming to face him, and I'm trying to build up my courage . . .' her voice trailed off weakly.

Max ran a gentle finger down her cheek, his touch making her heart beat faster, his body relaxed again.

'You'll find that courage, Jassy, I know you will. You'll have to fight, because Moreau wants you.' The last three words were bitten out almost savagely, and Jassy stared up at him, scanning his hard face curiously.

'No——' she denied, feeling panicky.

'Don't you underestimate him, he does want you,' Max repeated harshly. 'Any fool could see that just by watching him tonight.'

'I don't want to know!' Jassy cried, feeling almost sick. Max had just confirmed her worst fears about René, and although she believed him, she did not want to think about it. If Morgan and René had joined forces would she have any chance against them?

'I'm sorry, I didn't mean to frighten you.' Max's smile was warm, taking her breath away. He touched her face again. 'Tell me about you.'

Jassy laughed, her fears sternly pushed to the back of her mind in her determination to make the most of her time spent with this fascinating man.

'There's not much to tell. After my mother married Morgan, I was sent away to boarding school. I left last year and I wanted to get a job, but Morgan prefers me to be with him, and he travels so much that I couldn't hold down a job for long enough. I've started to paint, though, and I really enjoy it—I'll show you some of my paintings if you like.'

'I'd like that,' Max nodded. Then, 'How old are you, Jassy?' he asked, his voice hard and strange.

'Nineteen. Why?'

'I'm thirty-six,' he answered harshly, his mouth twisting almost bitterly. Jassy frowned, wondering what to say. She had not asked him his age, although she would have estimated mid-thirties. She turned away and wandered down to the sea edge, the water cool on her feet.

'Are you married?' she asked guilelessly, over her shoulder, praying with all her heart that the answer was no.

Max regarded her with amused eyes. 'No,' he replied crisply, strolling towards her with swift animal grace.

Very relieved, Jassy looked at him, her mouth dry as his wide shoulders blocked out the moonlight. His green eyes were glittering as they rested on the vulnerable curve of her mouth. Gazing into his lean, handsome face, she knew what he was thinking, and she wanted his kiss.

'Kiss me,' she breathed softly, her parted lips an invitation, her heart beating so heavily that she was deafened as he reached for her, his strong hands closing on her shoulders and pulling her close to him. She stared into his molten eyes, mesmerised as he lowered his head very slowly, his mouth warm and hard as he kissed her forehead, his lips then trailing across her closed eyelids.

The hands on her shoulders had slipped beneath the light cotton material of her loose caftan and were exploring her soft bare skin, tracing the hollow beneath her collar-bone, slowly. His mouth brushed her lips gently and Jassy began to tremble, lifting her hands to his shoulders to stop herself swaying against him, her fingers clenching as she felt his powerful muscles tightening.

His mouth was still teasing hers with small gentle kisses, coaxing her lips apart, and as her mouth opened, she heard him groan as his mouth finally took complete possession. His arms came around her, moulding her to the hard length of his muscular body, and his kiss deepened with passion as he slowly and sensuously explored the inner softness of her mouth for the first time.

Jassy was dizzy with the sensations he was arousing in her. Her heart was still beating crazily and her eyes were tightly closed as her fingertips brushed his thick hair, her pale arms tightening around his neck.

At that moment Max reluctantly lifted his head, breaking the kiss. He looked down at her with eyes that burned.

'Have some mercy on me, Jassy,' he muttered, breathing deeply, as he raked his hand through the darkness of his hair. Jassy smiled at him, her mouth swollen and vulnerable from his kiss, the like of which she had never experienced before. It had shattered all her romantic, childish illusions, awakening in her a pulsing fire that left her entire body weak and aching. She had been kissed before, of course, but had felt nothing, breaking away as soon as possible. The touch of Max's mouth had shot through her body like pain, arousing every part of her, every nerve from head to toe.

He watched her bemusedly touching her fingers to her lips, his eyes unfathomable. Then he smiled very gently, taking her hand and slowly kissing the palm.

'Time to get back, I think,' he murmured regretfully. 'Your stepfather will kill me with his bare hands if he finds out you've been with me!'

Although he was only joking, Jassy was brought down to earth with a bump, as she wrinkled her nose in disbelief. She had the distinct feeling that Morgan would be no match for Max Bellmer— under any circumstances.

And Max knew that.

CHAPTER THREE

THE phone was ringing, and Jassy shifted restlessly in her sleep, her eyes finally snapping open as she realised that the harsh, persistent sound was not a dream. She rolled sleepily out of bed and picked up the receiver.

'Mmm?' she murmured huskily, still too sleepy for her mind to form words, pushing back her tousled hair with a careless hand.

'Spend the day with me, Jassy.' Max Bellmer's deep, drawling voice sent a cold shiver down her warm, relaxed body and jerked her into an instant wide-awake awareness. The prospect of spending a whole day in his company was exciting, and she had no other plans—

'I don't know ... Morgan. . . .' she began cautiously, but Max did not give her time to finish.

'I'll pick you up outside your hotel in an hour,' he asserted, laughter threading his voice, and hung up.

Jassy stared at the receiver for a second, unable to contain the excited smile that curved her lips. She remembered how she had lain in bed for hours, the night before, waiting for sleep to claim her, her body still aching, her mouth still tingling from the touch of those beautifully sensual lips.

She had dreamt of him too, although she could not remember any of the dreams clearly.

The suite was quiet; Morgan was obviously still sleeping, which was not surprising, as there had been no sign of him before she had fallen asleep. She was loath to wake him, not examining her motives too closely, so she decided that if he had not surfaced by the time she left she would leave him a note, cowardly though that might be.

The next thing to do was to ring for coffee—she felt too nervous and excited to be able to face any food—and that done, she took a shower.

The water was deliciously cool, and after dusting herself with lightly-scented talc, Jassy slipped on a silk robe and sipped her rich, bitter coffee while deciding what to wear.

Ten minutes before she was due to meet Max she was dressed in a black bikini under jeans and a white peasant-style blouse which gave her a curiously fragile look. Her blonde hair swung thick and silky down her back and her small face was free of make-up, except for a couple of coats of waterproof mascara that shadowed and darkened her brown eyes.

She examined herself critically in the mirror, childishly wishing that she was more beautiful, from the top of her shining head to her sandalled feet. She would have to do, she thought wryly, slipping a thin gold bangle on to her wrist.

She crammed a towel into her voluminous shoulder bag and some suntan oil, just in case. Max had not specified what plans he had for the day, so she wanted to be ready for anything and everything.

It was time to go, so scrawling a hasty note to Morgan explaining what was happening, Jassy slung her bag over her shoulder, and taking a deep breath left the suite and walked quickly to the lift, not managing to quell the butterflies in her stomach.

She emerged into the still and glaring sunlight a moment or so later, to find herself staring at Max, who was leaning indolently against a low black open-top sports car scanning a Spanish newspaper with an air of suppressed impatience. Jassy was overwhelmed by his strength, his magnificence.

He lifted his proud dark head, sensing her approach, and their eyes met, with Jassy experiencing a shocking turning of her stomach. Narrowed green eyes slid over her slender body appraisingly, taking in her appearance and her loose, shining hair with a faint unreadable smile.

She stood in front of him now and her breath seemed to be locked inside her lungs, and she did not dare to meet those probing eyes.

'Good morning, Jassy.' His lips brushed her forehead briefly, warm, hard and unbearably casual.

'Hello.' Her voice was small and breathless and she felt unaccountably shy. 'I didn't know what we'd be doing—you didn't say, so I hope. . . .' Her need to break the awkward silence had prompted her to speak and her voice trailed off uneasily as she listened to the nonsense she was talking.

'You look perfect,' said Max, his voice hard. 'Beautiful and unbearably innocent. Let's go, shall we?'

He opened the car door for her and Jassy slid inside, feeling very foolish, sensing that he was angry in some way. She cursed herself for the stupid remarks she had made. He had probably thought she was fishing for compliments on her appearance, and her face flamed, as she prayed that the day would not be a disaster.

Max was beside her in the car, only inches away, watching her, and Jassy was desperately aware of him, of every small movement he made, and most of all of his lazy scrutiny.

He touched her soft hair gently, aware of her shyness, his mouth tightening as she flinched, unable to help herself. Her heart was beating very fast, and she longed with all her soul to be able to laugh and talk to him normally. But the words were sticking in her throat, her mind was a complete, agonising blank and she was too affected by his nearness. He was too strong and overpowering this morning, nothing like the gentle, sympathetic man who had held her on the moonlit beach, and she could not cope with him.

'Okay, what is it?' His voice was quite expressionless, and she heard the click of his lighter and seconds later smelt the fragrance of expensive tobacco.

Still finding herself unable to look at him, Jassy shrugged miserably. 'I'm sorry,' she whispered, aware of how unsuitable her answer was.

'Has something happened? Your stepfather?' he pursued, his voice softening as his glance rested on the sad hunch of her slim shoulders.

Jassy shook her head, turning herself to face him, ignoring the inner leaping of all her senses as she fixed her stare on his beautifully-moulded mouth.

'No, nothing like that. I haven't even seen Morgan,' she muttered weakly.

'Then what is it? Why are you so jumpy and nervous this morning?'

She did not answer.

'Do you think I'm going to kidnap you, or maybe force my unwanted attentions on you?' he asked softly, his eyes dangerous.

'No——' Her hasty, immediate answer gave her away, and she coloured brightly.

His mouth twisted mockingly. 'What a trusting child you are, then,' he said harshly, stubbing out his cigarette with violent ease.

Jassy lowered her head, feeling hurt and very sensitive. His cold, deliberately cruel remark had cut through her like a knife through butter.

Max sighed, his eyes on her downturned, vulnerable profile. 'God, I'm sorry, Jassy—I've been behaving like a swine. Forgive me? It's just that I've been waiting——' He broke off abruptly, changing his mind in mid-sentence. He tilted up her face gently and gave her a coaxing, devastating smile.

'Forgive me?' he repeated persuasively.

How could she not forgive him? she thought, as she felt the shy smile of her response, curving her mouth and lighting her trusting eyes.

'I'm sorry too. I just feel so shy sometimes,' she said, hoping that he understood. He did.

'What would you like to do this morning?' he asked with a hard, warm grin, releasing her chin and switching on the engine.

'You choose,' she responded brightly, feeling happy again.

'Shall we swim? I know a private cove farther along the shore.'

'It sounds perfect. I'm not feeling very energetic today and lying in the sun will suit me fine,' Jassy laughed.

As they pulled speedily on to the coast road, she glanced discreetly at the dark man sitting so near to her, careful not to let him become aware of her scrutiny.

He looked lean and tanned, his slim hips and powerful legs encased in faded blue denim jeans that stretched tight across his flat muscular stomach. He also wore a blue sleeveless tee-shirt that left bare his wide brown shoulders and strongly-muscled arms. Jassy watched with fascination, the rippling movements of those muscles, as he deftly manoeuvred the car along the busy coast road. He was very strong, a superb male animal and the leashed power that he unconsciously emitted made her skin prickle with tiny darts of excitement.

Her gaze moved upwards to his tanned throat and sharply-defined fleshless jaw, and the thick dark hair that lay against his neck, glinting in the relentless light, and her breathing became suddenly shallow and difficult. She remembered with heart-stopping clarity the touch and feel of his smooth, tanned skin,

the springy texture of the dark hair that matted his
flat chest, beneath her curling, sensitive fingertips,
when he had rescued her on the beach.

She had forgotten nothing of the feel or texture of
his body, it had haunted her dreams, branding her
mind with memory, and she shook her head now,
shocked by her emotive, perfect remembrance of
such tiny details.

Max Bellmer was becoming almost dangerous in
the way he was fast taking over all of her emotions.
She would have to tread carefully.

The car slid to a silent halt, breaking her thoughts
as she looked around at the small beautiful cove he
had brought her to. It was like a dream. A half-
moon of white deserted sand, sheltered by tall palm
trees and rioting, exotic vegetation, stretching to
clear lapping water. It was perfect.

Max was watching her with veiled perceptive eyes,
appreciating, through her easily-read shining face,
the beauty she saw before her.

She turned to him with eyes of soft velvet, honest
and innocent and happy. 'It's lovely,' she said
simply.

He nodded, flashing her a warm smile. 'Paradise,'
he agreed.

Out of the car, they picked their way through the
dry vegetation that was loud with humming, darting
insects, to the pale sand.

'How do you know this place, and why is it
empty?' Jassy asked curiously, throwing her bag on
to the sand, and kicking off her sandals.

'It's a private beach.' He pointed to a low white
villa that Jassy had not noticed, perched on the
brown barren rocks behind them. 'The villa belongs
to my sister and her husband,' he explained briefly.

Jassy stared at the house, that was clearly visible
from the beach. Flat-roofed and one storey high,

cool-looking cane blinds hung at the large modern windows and bright flowering vines clung to its outside walls. It was beautiful and she tried to imagine what it would be like to live in such a perfect place, remembering what Morgan had said about Max's sister being married to a Spaniard.

'Is your sister like you?' she asked, shading her eyes as she glanced into his dark face.

'You'll see for yourself, we're having lunch with her,' he replied laughingly.

'Oh! But I'm not dressed. . . .' she stammered, looking down at her jeans in dismay.

Max shook his head dismissively, ignoring her protest. 'You look perfect to me. Besides, Roxie doesn't stand on ceremony,' he laughed. 'You worry too much, Jassy my darling.' His green eyes teased her gently as he spoke, shielding some darker emotion that lay in the depths of his expression. 'Shall we go for a swim?'

He stripped off his tee-shirt with one fluidly graceful movement, leaving Jassy's startled eyes moving hungrily over his naked chest. He caught that look, his eyes narrowing, flaming in response, as they stared at each other, embarrassed colour washing up over Jassy's face again. She had not moved.

'Shall I turn my back?' he taunted softly, eyeing her fully dressed figure, reading her mind.

'Yes.' Her choking, one-word answer made him laugh out loud, as he turned away and strolled indolently towards the sea, the sunlight gleaming on the long, hard sweep of his brown back.

Jassy stared after him for a few seconds before hastily pulling off her blouse and sliding out of her jeans. She walked slowly down to the sea, enjoying the warmth of the sun on her skin and the sand beneath her feet. Max turned before she had taken more than half a dozen steps, some sixth sense telling

him of her approach, and Jassy had to fight to keep
her expression calm and tranquil as his dark intent
glance slid over her body, lingering on the swell of
her white breasts, barely covered by the tiny bikini
top, and her slightly curved smooth hips and pale
naked thighs.

He watched her unsmilingly every inch of the way,
until she stood right in front of him, dry-mouthed
and with a deep warm ache in her lower limbs that
could not be explained.

She had not mistaken his hunger, his devouring
stare, it was burning in his fierce green eyes as they
looked at each other. She drew a deep shaking
breath, amazed and elated by the barely controlled
desire she saw in him, and walked past him, down to
the water's edge, gasping as the cold water hit her
heated bare skin. She swam out strongly, listening to
the splash behind her as Max followed, and floating
on to her back she watched him cutting through the
clear water with speed and grace. He caught up with
her in seconds and floated alongside her, and they
both stared up at the sky, a cloudless piercing blue
that seemed limitless.

Jassy gave a small sigh of pure contentment,
ending in a squeal of startled laughter as Max
deliberately splashed her, the unexpected water
making her gasp. In return she kicked up a fountain
of water over him, delighting in his deep amused
laughter, then began to swim away, fearing retribu-
tion. His strong hand closing on her ankle pulled her
down into the water before she got a few feet away,
so swimming underwater she manoeuvred herself behind him, bobbing up to push his head down, the feel
of his thick wet hair on her palm, shivering through
her.

They played together like small innocent children,
as graceful and as carefree as dolphins, until, feeling
quite worn out, Jassy struck out for the beach. She

had gone only a couple of yards when Max surfaced right in front of her, the water falling like diamonds from his wide brown shoulders.

Jassy laughed delightedly, the amusement dying in her eyes as she looked at him, and caught the expression on his serious face. He reached for her, pulling her against the hard length of his body, his fingers sliding caressingly on her wet skin.

She lifted her face to his, her lips parting in welcome, her hands moving to his smooth tanned shoulders involuntarily. She heard him murmur her name before his mouth touched hers, cool and tasting of salt, her immediate response hardening his lips, deepening his kiss to a fierce passionate demand, as they clung together in the buoyant sea.

Jassy could not think coherently, the only sensations in the world at that moment were produced by Max's mouth and by his hands as they stroked the curved length of her back.

He was supporting her in the water, she was weightless, arching back her head in surrender as his mouth slid to her throat in exploration, a warm languourous aching sensation spreading through her body, at his cool loving touch.

Then she was free as Max released her, and she sank into the soothing water, filled with feelings and sensations that she had never known before, and wondering why he had let her go.

They swam back to the beach in warm, companionable silence, side by side, and Jassy threw herself down on the warm sand, tired but happy. The sun dried their wet bodies in seconds, leaving salt-bloomed skin, powdered by sand.

She lay very still and relaxed, her eyes closed against the glare of the sun, acutely aware that Max lay only inches away at her side, lazily propped up on one elbow, his watchful green eyes never leaving her face.

The gentle exertion of so much swimming had left her drowsy and lethargic, and she let herself drift towards sleep, recapturing in her mind the touch of Max's mouth and the erotic strokings of his brown hands.

She was almost asleep when his laughing voice jerked her back to consciousness.

'Sit up,' he ordered gently. 'You seem determined to burn yourself up.'

Jassy eased herself into a sitting position gracefully, and flashed him a shy smile.

'I always forget, it's a wonder I'm not burnt to a crisp,' she said, reaching into the shoulder bag for her bottle of suntan oil.

Max shook his head, silent with amusement, and took the bottle from her unresisting fingers, kneeling at her side, as he poured a small amount into the palm of his hand.

'I can manage, you know,' Jassy protested weakly, fighting her pleasure at the thought of the smooth stroke of his hands on her bare skin again.

'Can you?' His voice was significant, his eyes razor-sharp on her gentle, rounded profile. She knew what he was referring to.

'Max, I. . . .' she turned to him, the words sticking in her throat and refusing to move, at his nearness, his almost overpowering sexual magnetism. She could not meet his eyes, instead, her glance rested on his gleaming, muscular body, as she bit her lower lip nervously.

'Be still, Jassy,' Max advised softly, the low easy drawl accelerating her heartbeat.

She lifted her head, daring to meet his deep green eyes and seeing not interrogation or censure, but friendship and concern.

'You're right,' she giggled, realising how foolish

she had been. 'I'm not a contortionist!'

The tension was eased and his deep growl of answering laughter rang in her ears, making her shiver deliciously.

'Turn around,' said Max, suddenly businesslike.

Jassy did as she was told, lifting her wet hair from her shoulders. She experienced a moment of pure shock as his fingers eased the thin straps of her bikini top from her shoulders, her whole body stiffening, the touch of his casual fingers like fire on her skin, as an expectant excitement gripped her, like a vice.

'You're as nervous as a kitten,' he muttered against her ear, his cool breath fanning her hot cheeks gently.

'I'm not,' she whispered her lie, feeling slightly piqued that he was so damned perceptive.

'Well, relax, child. I may want you in my bed, but using half a bottle of suntan oil to get you there is overdoing it a little, don't you think?' Max teased her, coaxing away her nervousness easily and making her laugh.

The touch of his fingers, seconds later against her soft bare skin was light and soothing and showed no signs of desire.

He rubbed the oil gently over her shoulders, arms and back, his strong sensitive fingertips exploring and massaging slowly. Jassy closed her eyes, letting the sheer ecstasy of his touch wash over her, committing it to memory. Then, far too soon, it was over and Max was handing her the oil, grinning at her with warm lazy eyes.

'You'd better do the front,' he murmured wickedly, his lean face slashed into a devastating, unashamed smile.

Jassy glanced briefly into his glinting eyes and then, rather selfconsciously, covered the front of her body with a thin protective film of suntan oil. She held out the bottle to Max.

'Do you want some?'

He shook his head, the sun catching in his wet hair. 'I don't burn,' he said softly, and again Jassy sensed the hidden significance of his words, without understanding.

She lay back on the warm sand utterly contented. She could not imagine being happier, it was a beautiful, perfect day to be spent in the company of a man who intrigued her more and more as she got to know him.

She glanced discreetly through her lashes and saw him lying beside her, his hands behind his head, his hard, hair-roughened chest moving steadily up and down to the rhythm of his breathing. He was staring up into the sky, seemingly preoccupied, and just to look at him made Jassy's pulses leap, and she wondered about him.

She turned on to her stomach, unaware of her provocative grace, and looked at him openly.

'Do you enjoy being wealthy and powerful?' she asked candidly, her soft eyes meeting his questioningly.

'How do you know that I'm wealthy and powerful?' he parried in a low drawl, his green eyes faintly teasing.

'It's obvious,' Jassy replied seriously. 'Not only by looking at you but also because Morgan was very interested in you last night, and he isn't interested in anybody who isn't wealthy and powerful.'

Max looked at her speculatively for a moment, then shrugged, his broad shoulders lifting with indifferent grace.

'I enjoy certain aspects of my business, obviously, or I wouldn't do it. The wealth and the power are merely the emblems of my own success at that business. Mind you,' he laughed, 'that isn't to say that I don't enjoy money, it makes life a hell of a lot easier.'

Jassy considered his answer carefully, liking what it showed of his personality. He did not seem obsessed as Morgan was, with business and power and the endless cut and thrust of making vast amounts of money, although she was under no illusions about the hard ruthless streak that ran through him. She had seen it in his face when he had been talking to Morgan and Pierre, and a man could not rise to Max's powerful, wealthy position without a certain amount of ruthless intent. He was an enigma and she wanted to know more about him.

'Are you from a rich family?' she asked next.

'Why don't you ask your stepfather?' he asked mockingly.

Jassy flushed, knowing full well that Morgan would know all about Max Bellmer, and Max was under no illusions about that.

'I'm sorry, I didn't mean to pry,' she said sadly, her face still hot.

Max frowned, realising how easily hurt she was. 'You're not prying, and I'm sorry for my careless choice of words. I know your stepfather is a sore point at the moment.'

Jassy nodded ruefully. 'This has nothing to do with Morgan anyway. I was only asking about you because I'm interested, you seem . . . I don't know. . . .' Her voice trailed off, leaving her embarrassed.

'I seem what?' Max asked with interest.

Jassy shook her head silently. She had said too much, she was sure, but she had felt the need to set the record straight. She could not let Max think that her interest in him had been fostered or suggested in any way, by Morgan. She was not involved in any of Morgan's business transactions and she needed Max to know that once and for all.

'I . . . I just wanted you to know that it's nothing

to do with Morgan, but with me, that's all.' She
glanced at him anxiously to find him staring at her
in that intent, probing way she was becoming used
to.

He reached out and stroked her cheek with a tan-
talising finger.

'I get the message,' he murmured, understanding
her, his face almost tender as he looked at her. She
wrinkled her nose at him.

'You can tell me about yourself, then,' she retorted
smilingly, the sun catching her hair and turning it
into a brilliant halo around her sweet face.

'There's not much to tell,' said Max, squinting
against the sun, his eyes on the distant hazy horizon.
'Roxie and I were orphaned when we were kids and
brought up on the wrong side of New York by my
mother's sister. She was poor, so we worked to pay
for our education, and as soon as I could, I rented
an apartment for the two of us, and we moved out of
our aunt's. That's it—I have an easy life now, and
so does Roxie, things have turned out well for both
of us. Poverty is a great spur.' He laughed without
bitterness, easily glossing over what Jassy could see
had been a hard, poor and difficult upbringing. She
would never have guessed because he had the
polished dignity that usually accompanied wealth
from birth, and her new knowledge lent him even
more fascination in her eyes. She wanted to pester
him with questions about himself, to find out everything about him, but she managed to restrain herself,
silently watching him placing a cigarette between
his lips and lighting it with practised ease. He offered
her one which she refused, her eyes riveted on the
thin curls of smoke being exhaled from his nostrils,
and then she turned her head away, realising how
she had been staring.

Every tiny movement he made seemed to hold

her spellbound, capturing every last ounce of her attention, and she found that she could not dismiss him, even for a split-second, from her thoughts. She was inexorably drawn to him. It was all very strange and new, this feeling for a man, and she felt a little confused.

'Are you asleep, Jassy?' She had been lying very still, her head turned away from him, as she wrestled with her thoughts, trying to sort out her strong, jumbled feelings for him, but his quietly-spoken question swivelled her head round towards him again.

'Maybe,' she answered cryptically, wondering in fact if it was all a dream. It certainly seemed too good to be true that he had asked her to spend the day with him. Would she wake up in a moment to find herself in bed, in her hotel room?

Max smiled at her. 'My life story usually has that effect on people. What goes on in that beautiful little head of yours?' he asked indulgently.

Jassy shrugged, her expression that of a temptress. 'I'm not telling you,' she retorted impishly.

'Tell me about your childhood, then. I've already revealed the dreadful secrets of the Bellmer family, so it's your turn,' he said, with curious persuasive eyes on her upturned face.

'I think I told you most of it last night. When my mother married Morgan I was sent away to boarding school as soon as possible. I suppose I was lonely, and a little envious of all my friends who had real families. I remember that I always wanted a brother—an older brother, I think. I used to go to visit Lavender, my best friend, in the holidays. She had two brothers and two sisters, and their house always seemed happy and alive. . . .' Her voice was wistful with memory, until she pulled herself together. 'I'm probably giving you the wrong impression. I was happy and I know that boarding school gave me an independence that I'm glad for now. When my mother died, I only had Morgan left. He's been like a father to me, and that's why this whole situation with René is so difficult. Oh dear, I'm sorry—this must be dreadfully boring for you,' she said apologetically, realising that she had been chattering on.

Max was staring at her, and he shook his head.

'I asked, remember? What about boy-friends, is there anyone special?' he asked carefully.

Jassy tossed back her hair, feeling a little embarrassed.

'No—I haven't had much time for boy-friends. I travel around with Morgan and he's terribly protective, and also, he vets all the men I meet. He seems determined to marry me off to somebody who'll help the business.' She stopped suddenly, clamping her hand over her mouth in a charmingly childlike gesture, her gentle brown eyes widening with shock and worry. 'I shouldn't be telling you all this, it seems disloyal to Morgan somehow. Perhaps you would forget what I've said?' she pleaded.

Max laughed aloud. 'Don't worry, child, I won't use anything you tell me against you.' He was gently mocking her.

'You seem to be able to elicit my confidence very easily,' Jassy said wonderingly. 'Will we be friends?'

'I think not,' Max replied, deadly serious. 'I want more than friendship from you, Jassy. You should know that by now.' His voice had become very soft, an insidious caress, and his glittering eyes rested on her mouth as he spoke.

A second later, with one lightning, easy movement, he arched over her relaxed body, holding her prisoner against the hot sand.

Jassy, dry-mouthed, stared into the burning

depths of his eyes, mesmerised by something she saw in them, until he lowered his head, in slow motion it seemed, blotting out all light as their mouths touched with a startling explosion that sent exquisite, fiery sensations flooding through her.

Max's kiss was hungry, making no concession to her innocence or inexperience, as he plundered the sweetness of her mouth, passionately, demanding her total response, her total surrender.

His hands moved in restless sensual caress against the heated bare skin of her waist, the touch of her body accelerating his heartbeat against her breasts.

Jassy felt dizzy as his warm hard body pressed down on hers, making her achingly conscious of every tiny irrelevant detail of him—the short crisp hairs on his chest, rough against her skin, the hard warmth of his thighs against hers.

She coiled her arms around his neck, letting her fingers play through the thick dark vitality of his hair, as his mouth moved against hers in endless coaxing expertise, and the potent strength of his body pinned her beneath him.

Max broke the kiss, a moment later, and with a hoarse groan slid his arms beneath her and rolled on to his back, pulling her on top of him, so that their positions were reversed. He smiled into her face, his eyes still burning with unconcealed desire, but his heavy body suddenly taut and well under control.

'Oh, Jassy,' he murmured huskily against her white throat. 'You drive me crazy—your skin is so soft, you're so beautiful.'

Jassy lifted her head and pressed her mouth to his lean brown cheek in a gentle caress. Her heart was still beating erratically and a warm languorous weakness was melting her limbs. She wanted to tell him that she loved him, that no man had ever made her feel this way before, but she kept silent, sensing

that it was not the right time for such confessions.
He probably knew anyway.

A sense of power and elation filled her. Max
wanted her, that fact was beyond doubt, and he had
drawn back, using iron self-control, for her sake.

'Are you hungry?' Max questioned gently,
threading his fingers through her tousled hair and
pushing it back from her face, touching his warm
mouth to the throbbing pulse in her throat.

'Starving!' Jassy admitted breathlessly, the touch
of his mouth shuddering through her, as always. He
lifted his arm with lazy grace and glanced at his
watch.

'Time for lunch, I think.' He pulled her to her
feet, holding her within the strong circle of his arms
for a moment, crushing her tightly against him, in
need he did not bother to disguise.

Jassy laid her own arms around his waist, pressing
her cheek to his smooth brown shoulder, longing for
his kiss, longing for his love.

They dressed and strolled hand in hand towards
the low white villa.

CHAPTER FOUR

'Hi, Max! And you must be Jassy—welcome!' With a tremendous upsurge of relief, Jassy recognised, within a split second, the woman who greeted them as the same woman she had seen stepping from Max's car, in the town the day before. She was a tall, slender woman in her late twenties, her thick, shiny hair as dark as her brother's. She also had the same green eyes, although the expression in them was delightfully feminine, and a small, triangular face. Dressed in fashionable white trousers and a patterned, cotton blouse she looked cool and chic and very attractive. Best of all, she was Max's sister, and consequently Jassy's smile was radiant as she held out her hand.

'Hello, I'm very pleased to meet you, Mrs. . . .' She realised that she did not know the woman's surname.

'Call me Roxanne, I insist.' She had the same soft American drawl as Max, and the hand that gripped Jassy's was firm and slender.

'Max has told me all about you,' Roxanne remarked, with a friendly, open smile, her eyes candidly assessing Jassy's cascading golden hair and superb figure. 'And I see that he wasn't exaggerating—you're beautiful. Sit down, please,' she waved a casual hand towards the finely-wrought patio chairs, 'and let me fix you a drink. What would you like?'

'Dubonnet, please,' Jassy smiled, feeling drawn to this dark vivacious lady, who had turned out to be Max's sister.

'Scotch for you, Max?' Roxanne questioned busily.

'Hey, slow down, Roxie! You wear me out, just watching you.' Max smiled lazily, catching his sister by the arm as she tried to bustle past him, and lowering his dark gleaming head to press his lips to her forehead.

Roxanne laughed, an attractive tinkle of amusement, and returned his kiss.

Jassy watched the easy familiarity and the obvious love between them, with a slight pang of envy, realising, as she did sometimes in the company of others, just how lonely it was being an only child. If she ever had any children, she decided firmly, she would definitely have at least two.

Would Max's children inherit his green, tiger eyes and saturnine good looks? she wondered, letting her dreamy gaze rest on the proud tilt of his head as he fondly watched Roxanne pouring out the drinks. A flush crept up her face at the intimacy of her thoughts. Max's children—was she going mad? She hardly knew him.

'Sit down, Max,' Roxanne ordered with a smile, handing him a glass of Scotch with ice.

'Yes, ma'am,' came the deep, amused reply as he coiled his lean muscular frame into one of the white patio chairs near to Jassy.

Roxanne handed Jassy her drink, also liberally iced, and sat down beside her.

'Tomás will be out in a moment,' she explained. 'He was held up by a call from the States—he's just showering.'

'Your husband?' Jassy asked with a smile.

Roxanne nodded. 'Always business,' she said, lifting her hands in a fatalistic gesture that was not quite serious.

Jassy and Max both laughed.

'I know exactly what you mean,' Jassy said expressively, thinking about her stepfather.

'That came straight from the heart. Has my brother been giving you a hard time?' Roxanne teased.

'Oh no ... no ...' Jassy replied quickly, cursing the tell-tale colour that had rushed to her face, and caught Roxanne's curious eye.

'Where's Rafael?' Max suddenly cut in smoothly, cleverly averting attention from Jassy's obvious embarrassment.

'Sleeping in his room, thank goodness!' Roxanne replied, unable to keep the gentleness out of her eyes, even though she tried to sound thankful. Max caught Jassy's curiosity and explained, 'Rafael is Roxie's young son, my one and only nephew.'

'How old is he?' Jassy turned shining eyes on Roxanne, her love of children obvious.

'Eighteen months. Would you like to see him?'

'Oh, yes, please!'

Max listened to the enthusiasm in her voice and watched her with hooded enigmatic eyes as she jumped to her feet with youthful grace.

The two women strolled into the cool, dim house and Jassy gazed around with interest. The slatted wooden shutters were closed against the glare of the midday sun, and the thin lines of light they admitted left the interior of the villa deliciously cool and dark.

They passed through the lounge, silent except for the faint hum of the air-conditioning system, their sandalled feet clicking on the black marble floor.

'What a beautiful room!' Jassy exclaimed, taking in the pale walls and light modern furniture, the whole design of the room, simple yet stunning.

Roxanne smiled. 'Thank you.' She was obviously pleased by Jassy's compliments.

They strolled through a heavy wooden door into

a light, airy hallway, and quietly opening one of the many doors leading off it, Roxanne beckoned Jassy into a small room.

Again the shutters were closed, but there was enough light for Jassy to appreciate the warm, peach-coloured walls, and the scattered toys and pictures that made it a child's room.

In the centre of the room stood a huge crib, made from dark carved wood and covered with filmy lace. Peeping inside, Jassy caught sight of Rafael.

He was a beautiful child and she stood spellbound, filled with wonder as she looked at his tiny, perfectly-formed hands and the fluffy dark down that was his hair. A soft smile curved her vulnerable mouth.

'He's beautiful,' she breathed to Roxanne, her eyes still lingering on the rounded curve of the child's incredibly soft-skinned face.

Roxanne's eyes were proud and loving as they tiptoed from the room, and joined Max on the patio.

Another man sat with him. Tall and handsome with tanned skin and dark flashing eyes, it was Tomás, Roxanne's husband. Both men got to their feet and as Jassy was introduced to Tomás, he lifted her hand to his lips with an old-fashioned, charming gesture.

'Welcome to our home, Jassy,' he said with a smile, his English perfect, with only a very slight accent.

Jassy smiled back, liking the tall, polite Spaniard, her face still soft and gentle as she thought of Rafael.

'Thank you. You must be very proud of your son,' she said huskily, aware that Max's green eyes were narrowed in close scrutiny on her face.

'Of course. Although he is quite a handful.' Tomás laughed, curling his arm around Roxanne's shoulder. Jassy watched them together. They were obviously very much in love, and there seemed to be a special and private communication that passed between them constantly, like electricity. I wonder if people will look at me one day and be able to tell how much in love I am, she wondered. Most of all, Roxanne and Tomás had Rafael, the product of their love, and Jassy could imagine nothing more beautiful.

Lost in her own thoughts, she looked up absently to find Max staring at her. He was sitting opposite to her, a couple of feet away, smoking idly, his broad, powerful shoulders gleaming in the relentless light.

'What are you thinking about?' he asked gently, his eyes filled with amused indulgence, his mouth a straight line of hungry intensity, as he gazed at her faraway face.

Bringing her thoughts down to earth, she saw that they were quite alone on the patio. She could hear Roxanne and Tomás laughing together just inside the house.

'I was just thinking how much in love your sister and her husband are, and how lucky they are to have such a beautiful life together,' she answered honestly, not quite able to meet his eyes, and wondering why.

'Have you ever been in love, Jassy?' He was still staring at her, unnerving her.

'No, but I can imagine what it's like.' You've taught me that, she added to herself silently. She glanced up at him. 'What about you?'

'Once, I've been in love once,' he replied, his voice suddenly harsh, the kind indulgence gone from his eyes, to be replaced by a brooding intensity. His brief answer shook Jassy more than she could have imagined, and she felt as though an unseen hand was squeezing her heart painfully. Did he still love this unknown lady? She had a thousand painful questions to ask, but a surreptitious glance at his hard, veiled profile told her that he would not speak of it.

The silence grew between them until Roxanne appeared carrying a laden tray. Jassy jumped to her feet, profoundly grateful for the diversion.

'Can I help?' she asked, but Roxanne shook her dark head.

'It's ready. I thought we'd eat out here.' She placed the tray on the table and began unloading it, deftly setting four places.

Tomás appeared with the wine and a few moments later they were all sitting around the table tucking into a hard-boiled egg and leek salad. It was quite delicious, and Jassy ate with relish. Having missed breakfast, she had not realised just how hungry she was.

Max's good humour seemed to have returned as he chatted to Tomás and teased Roxanne. Jassy listened mostly, throwing in a comment now and again, but it was heavenly just to sit out in the open air, shaded from the bright sun, fanned by the faint fresh breeze from the ocean, opposite the most fascinating and attractive man she had ever met.

The main course was devilled crab, a speciality of Roxanne's, Jassy learned, and after the fresh fruit and cheese that was dessert, they all sat back replete, sipping thick sweet coffee.

Jassy's small sigh of happiness drew Max's attention, a faint smile curving his hard mouth as he offered her a cigarette. She took one, returning his smile, and her hand shook a little as it curved over his to shield from the breeze the light he extended.

'Thank you.' Her voice was huskily polite, as she tried to ignore the sudden flare of light in his eyes.

Jassy insisted on helping Roxanne with the washing up, leaving the two men to talk together. Max was too overpowering and it was a perfect opportunity to get away from him for a while, to regain the composure that he could so easily destroy with nothing more than a casual glance.

The kitchen was small and very compact, equipped with all the modern conveniences and painted a bright cheerful yellow.

The two women chatted companionably, the first bonds of friendship forming easily, as Roxanne washed and Jassy dried the lunch dishes. Jassy had learned over lunch that Roxanne and Tomás only used this villa as a holiday home.

'Where do you usually live?' she asked curiously now, carefully drying a flower-patterned plate.

'For most of the year, we live in Madrid,' Roxanne replied. 'The head office of Tomás' company is there, although we always spend a few months here—usually in the summer.'

'You're very lucky—it's beautiful,' Jassy agreed. 'Do you speak Spanish?' she asked, wondering at the difficulties of living in a foreign country permanently.

'A little,' Roxanne laughed. 'Lucky for me that Tomás speaks such perfect English. What about you?'

Jassy shook her head. 'None, I'm afraid. I took French and German at school, but I'm not too good at those. I think you have to have a special aptitude for languages.'

'School? How old are you, Jassy, if you don't mind me asking.'

'I'm nineteen, nearly twenty, and I don't mind you asking.'

Roxanne laughed. 'No wonder Max looks at you like a hungry wolf!'

'I don't understand.' Jassy stared at Roxanne with confused eyes.

'You're very young, he's probably scared to touch you. I know the way Max's mind works and he'll be thinking that he's old enough to be your father.'

'Oh dear!' Jassy's voice held a wealth of meaning, her dismay patently obvious. 'Do you really think so?'

'Oh, Jassy, I'm sorry—I've upset you, and I could bite my tongue out. I have this terrible habit of putting my foot in my mouth. You're very fond of Max, aren't you?'

'Yes,' Jassy admitted shyly. 'I've never met anybody like him before. But you haven't upset me, Roxanne—honestly. It just hadn't occurred to me that Max might think that way. I don't think age matters at all, do you?' she hastened to reassure the other woman, not letting her mind dwell too much on what had been said. She would work it all out later when she was alone. At present it was enough that Max sought her company.

'I'm sure it doesn't matter. Tomás is fourteen years older than me, but it doesn't make the slightest difference, we don't even think about it,' Roxanne said brightly.

Jassy digested this, feeling hopeful.

'Tell me more about your life, I'm fascinated.'

Roxanne gave her a last searching look before answering the question, a faint frown pleating her smooth tanned brow, still worried that she had offended the younger girl.

'Well, as I said, our home is in Madrid, and we also have a house in England and an apartment in New York.'

'Don't you miss America?' Jassy asked curiously. She had not realised how wealthy Roxanne and Tomás were.

'I fly over to the States about twice a year, so I don't really miss it. Besides, New York is no place to bring up a child.' Jassy nodded sympathetically, and Roxanne continued, 'My life is with Tomás and Rafael—I don't care where I live as long as I'm with them.'

'I envy you, you're very lucky,' Jassy said wistfully.

Roxanne smiled. 'Yes, I guess I am. There, all finished.' The last glass was dried and stored away.

'Thanks for the lunch, it was delicious,' said Jassy.

'I'm glad you came. I was dying to meet you,' Roxanne admitted candidly.

Jassy wondered what Max had said about her, but quelled the urge to ask his sister, as they strolled outside to join the men.

Jassy's eyes flew to Max as soon as he came in sight, her heartbeat quickening, a sensation she was fast becoming used to, as she let her eyes rest hungrily on him.

He was talking to Tomás in Spanish, his fluency somehow not surprising her, his smile charming, his green eyes veiled yet amused. As she watched, he raked an impatient brown hand through the glinting vitality of his thick black hair, the indolent grace of that casual, unconscious action riveting Jassy's glance. Sensing her watchful stare, he turned his head towards her and she immediately lowered her eyes, unable to hide the faint colour that stained her cheeks.

Both men got to their feet as the women stepped on to the patio, and Jassy found herself dry-mouthed and tongue-tied as Max slid a muscled arm around her shoulder and hugged her against him for a second, as though he had missed her. He smiled down at her, his eyes slowly sweeping the young, vulnerable curve of her neck and the rapid rise and fall of her breasts, then he released her and, feeling desperately short of breath, she sank into a chair, taking the cigarette offered by Roxanne with quivering fingers and drawing on it deeply until some semblance of normality returned.

The afternoon passed quickly and pleasantly. They sat in the sun and sipped long cool drinks, the talk light and amusing. Jassy's eyes strayed to the tall powerful man sitting next to her, times without number, unable to stop herself. In his turn, Max watched her steadily and intently, a tense, hungry awareness building up between them.

Jassy was again aware of every small movement he made, the casual lifting of an expressive hand, the slight shifting of a muscled leg, even the deep, steady intake of his breath. Every sense she had was filled with him, and she ached low in her stomach.

As she caught his eye for the umpteenth time, her heart stopped beating for an agonising second, as their glances locked. Flame leapt in Max's green eyes before the contact was broken, flame that burned and seared its message into Jassy's body and mind. This tiny episode lasted only an instant, totally unnoticed by Roxanne and Tomás, but it seemed to Jassy to have lasted for timeless hours.

And so it continued all afternoon, building up and building up, a never-ending spiral of broken eye-contact and tingling desire, until Max got to his feet with lightning grace, lazily stretching his taut brown arms above his head.

'Time for us to go, Jassy,' he drawled, with a smile.

Jassy got to her feet immediately, smiling at Roxanne and Tomás.

'Thank you for a lovely afternoon,' she said quietly.

'Come again soon,' said Roxanne, kissing her cheek. 'And you, Max.'

Jassy watched as Max enfolded Roxanne in his

strong arms and kissed her forehead.

'Take care, Roxie, I'll call you,' he promised. He shook hands with Tomás and then, taking Jassy's hand, strolled across the beach towards the low sports car.

She walked beside him contentedly, aware of his thumb caressing her small hand engulfed in his.

The sun was beginning to lose its heat and the sky was tinged with pink at its corners, the air a little cooler at last. Max's body seemed still and straight, vaguely aloof as they walked, and wondering at his sudden remoteness, she did not see the clump of weeds that caught her foot until it was too late and she stumbled forward, reaching for him involuntarily as she lost her balance.

He caught her easily, lifting her bodily, and placing her on her feet in front of him.

'Are you all right?' he asked quietly, scanning her face watchfully.

'Yes, I just tripped in those weeds,' Jassy answered breathlessly, wishing that she didn't sound so inane.

His hands still rested on her arms and as she looked up into his unfathomable eyes, his fingers tightened on her soft flesh, drawing her closer. One hand slid upwards to cup her face, his thumb moving rhythmically against the side of her mouth, his eyes darkening as he stared down at her.

Then he bent his head and touched his mouth to hers, his hard lips parting as they tasted the sweetness of her mouth.

He strained her closer, trapping her hands flat against his broad, flat chest, as the tension between them burst into flames and consumed them both.

Jassy could feel the heavy thunder of his heart as it began to race beneath her fingers, her own heart matching it, beat for beat. Her lips moved tantalisingly beneath the fierce invasion of his and she moaned his name, as his restless, urgent hands slid beneath the elasticated waistband of her thin blouse to move against her bare skin in slow, coaxing caress, making her tremble violently as he moulded her even closer to the hard taut length of his body.

His burning, hungry mouth moved slowly to her sensitive throat, and she arched against him, deafened by the roaring of her blood and the frenzy of her heartbeats.

She had never experienced such sweet, piercing, overwhelming desire and it made her weak and yielding as Max's warm, arousing fingers stroked up her body to find the soft swellings of her breasts.

Her flimsy bikini top was no barrier to his seeking hands and a second later she was shuddering with pleasure so sharp and so intense, it was almost pain, as those gentle brown fingers brushed endlessly and delicately over her sensitive nipples, hardening them and making her clench her hands into his smooth unyielding shoulders.

'Jassy——' Her name came from his mouth in a deep, hoarse whisper and his hands became still on her trembling body.

She opened her eyes slowly and stared up into his, meeting the dark heated desire she saw there with a small aching sigh. Max stared down at her, at the tousled golden hair that fell softly over his muscular arms, at the innocence of her bruised mouth, at the yielding slenderness of her body, and he closed his eyes, letting out a long shaking breath.

He released her, and she stood alone, swaying a little, a question shining in her eyes.

'I've been waiting all afternoon, for ever, to do that,' he said huskily.

She knew what he meant, because she had felt the same way, but why had he let her go? He saw the question and the traces of hurt in her face and slid an arm around her shoulder.

'Oh, Jassy,' he whispered, holding her gaze. 'You drive me to the very brink . . . do you know that? I couldn't sleep last night, after having you in my arms, but. . . .' He broke off with a graceful shrug of his shoulders and reached for his cigarettes, lighting one for her and placing it between her lips. Jassy drew on it, wondering what he had been about to say. She felt confused, but more than that, she was longing for him to take her back into his arms again. He was staring at her as she battled with her thoughts.

'You're so young, so innocent. I'm too old for you,' he said suddenly, his voice harsh, his face dark with self-reproach.

Jassy's head flew up. 'I don't think you're too old. And I can't help my age,' she said sadly, relieved at least that it was not because he did not want her.

'I guess not,' Max conceded drily.

She glared at him, convinced that he was making fun of her, and caught the slight smile in his green eyes.

'Pig!' she said, sticking out her tongue at him.

He laughed aloud, throwing back his dark head in open amusement, and Jassy had to laugh too.

The last of the tension and frustration dissolved with their laughter, as they reached the car. Max opened the door for her, then slid in himself and switched on the engine.

'Will you have dinner with me tonight?' he asked, loath to let her go, to let their day together end. He turned in his seat as he spoke.

She wanted to, so very much, but thoughts of Morgan intruded in her mind.

'I don't know . . . Morgan. . . .' she began, her disappointment lowering her head.

'To hell with Morgan!' Max said angrily, his

eyes possessive as he violently stubbed out his cigarette. Then, 'I'm sorry, Jassy, I just don't want to let you go tonight.' His eyes caressed her, his low, cool voice persuaded her.

Jassy smiled. 'I'll have to go back to shower and change,' she capitulated Morgan would understand. It was only one evening after all, out of all the evenings she spent with him. But despite this convincing of herself, she still felt apprehension gnawing at her, as the car glided almost silently on to the coast road, and headed back towards her hotel.

Max arranged to pick her up in two hours' time, touching his mouth briefly yet passionately to hers, when they reached her hotel.

Getting out of the car, she swung her bag on to her shoulder and smiled at him.

'Goodbye,' she said lightly. It was ridiculous, but she did not want to leave him.

'I'll see you later, Jassy,' he said gently.

She turned away, aware that he watched her every movement until she disappeared within the huge smoked-glass doors of her hotel.

The roar of the sports car's engine told her that he had gone, and she walked towards the lifts feeling unaccountably lonely. She prayed that Morgan would not be angry, crossing her fingers childishly as the lift carried her, all too quickly, up to her suite.

Her hand on the door knob trembled slightly, and noticing this, she drew a deep breath and stiffened her spine. There was no reason in the world why she should not accept a dinner invitation. She wasn't a child. Why should Morgan object? Max Bellmer was an extremely eligible man, to say nothing of his being more wealthy and infinitely more powerful than René. Morgan would surely approve of that, she thought with uncharacteristic cynicism.

But as she strolled into the suite, she knew that

she was wrong. Morgan was waiting for her, his cold eyes angry. Flinging aside the papers he had been working on, he got to his feet.

'Where the hell have you been all day?' he demanded furiously, his face a dull red colour.

'Didn't you get my note?' Jassy asked mildly, trying to mask her nervousness as she flung her bag casually onto a chair. She must not let Morgan bully her.

'I got a scrap of paper informing me that you intended to spend the day with Bellmer,' Morgan replied coldly.

Jassy shrugged. 'You know where I've been, then. Oh, please don't be angry, Morgan, I had a lovely day.' She smiled at him beseechingly, trying to coax him into a better mood. But her stepfather was not to be coaxed.

'Have you no sense of responsibility?' he snapped. His voice was becoming louder and more annoyed, and despite her promise to herself not to lose her temper, Jassy could feel her irritation growing at his unjust attitude.

'Oh, for goodness' sake, Morgan, I've just spent an extremely enjoyable day out with a friend. There's no crime in that, is there?'

'Friend?' Morgan pounced on the word. 'He's old enough to be your father. It's blatantly obvious what he wants from you, and it has nothing to do with friendship!' Her stepfather had lost his temper completely now, his words becoming ugly and uncontrolled.

Jassy stared at him with horror, feeling sick at the implications of his angry words.

'I don't wish to talk about it any more,' she said stiffly, her eyes flashing fury as she began to walk towards her bedroom. She would not be able to get through to Morgan until his temper had cooled.

A second later she found her exit blocked.

'Well, that's too bad, because I want to get this sorted out, once and for all, without your damned insolence,' Morgan said tightly, his mouth a cruel white line.

Jassy sighed. 'What is there to sort out?' she asked wearily. 'I've been out for the day and that's all there is to it. It's too late to change anything that's happened today. I'm sorry if you think I've been insolent, I certainly didn't intend to be.'

Morgan ignored her apology. 'René was here this afternoon. . . .' he began, but the telephone began to ring, cutting short the conversation. Morgan glanced at his watch as he answered the phone, barking a few angry words into the receiver and slamming it down almost immediately.

' 'I have to go out. I'll speak to you when I get back, young lady.' His tone brooked no argument and he did not even glance at her as he left the suite, violently banging the door shut behind him.

Jassy felt a prickle of hot tears behind her eyes as she sank into a chair, almost unaware of her actions.

Morgan's cruel words had shattered the happiness of her day, and slow sad tears began coursing down her pale face. How could he be so nasty? What had she done that was so very wrong? Time spent without his permission, she supposed, and the situation was getting out of hand.

Finally her tears dried and she wondered about cancelling her dinner date with Max. But she did not want to, and furthermore, she did not know how to get in touch with him. Her decision not to cancel brought a warm smile to her face as she dashed into the bathroom to shower.

Damn Morgan for being so possessive and so unreasonable! She would try her best not to let him spoil her evening, and the consequences would have to be faced later, not now.

Stepping from the cold shower, her body tingling, she dried her hair with a portable hair-dryer, and that done, she let the towel drop from her body and stared at herself in the full-length mirror in her bedroom. She was becoming lightly tanned, her skin the colour of pale honey, which was pleasing because it suited her.

The sun had also bleached her thick hair lighter, strands of it almost silver against her bare shoulders. Glancing over her body, she wrinkled up her small nose with dissatisfaction. Her rounded breasts, narrow waist and curved hips were distinctly unfashionable and she yearned, unaware of her own sensual attraction, for the slender boyish figure that no amount of dieting could give her.

With her eyes catching the clock she saw that she had a little over half an hour to get ready, and quickly slipped into cool, silky underwear, her dissatisfaction pushed to one side as she began to make up her face.

She never wore much make-up, but tonight she wanted to look special, so leaving her flawless complexion free of foundation and powder, she concentrated on her eyes, stroking gold shadow on to her eyelids and darkening her lashes with mascara. Richly-coloured lip gloss completed her make-up.

She pinned up her hair in an elegant knot, the severity of the style enhancing the superbly delicate bone structure of her face and the long vulnerable grace of her bared neck. This style also made her look older, she thought with satisfaction, the last thing she wanted was for Max to think that she was too young.

The dress she finally chose was of poppy-red cotton threaded with thin strands of gold. A fashionable gypsy style with a low, rounded neck and flaring skirt, it suited her to perfection, lending her a certain exotic charm. Swinging gold earrings and high-heeled red sandals completed her outfit, and she was just collecting a gauzy shawl in a contrasting shade of red, when a sharp rap on the door heralded Max's punctual arrival.

Breathing deeply in a vain attempt to slow the sudden acceleration of her heart, Jassy walked slowly to the door and opened it, her stomach turning over at the sight of the tall dark man who stood outside.

He was dressed formally and perfectly, in a dark green velvet dinner jacket, expensively cut to mould his broad shoulders and powerful chest. Jassy's eyes lingered for a second on his lean tanned face, his narrowed, unfathomable expression, before veering away in sudden tingling shock, to rest safely on his jacket.

'Hello, Max,' she said huskily, feeling painfully shy and lost for words.

'Hello, Jassy.' His voice was slumbrous, deep and cool. She could feel his slow and thorough inspection of her as surely as if he was touching her. 'You're incredibly beautiful,' he said at last in a gentle voice.

She steeled herself to look into his lazy green eyes, reading the truth of his husky compliment.

'Thank you.' Her smile was radiant.

'Shall we go?' He took her hand, and they walked to the lift together, down and out of the hotel into the dark balmy evening air. She did not look at him, fixing her eyes straight ahead, cursing once again her inability to chat easily, and longing for him to kiss her, touch her, reassure her.

But Max too was silent, seemingly preoccupied as they reached his car. Their eyes met as he opened the door for her, and long, sensitive fingers reached out to trace the soft line of her jaw.

'Why so silent, child?' he asked huskily, a smile playing at the corners of his mouth.

Jassy swallowed, dry-mouthed. 'I don't know what to say,' she admitted honestly, drowning in the warmth she saw in his eyes.

'Am I such an ogre?' he asked, almost seriously. His intent glance caught and held on the small perfect white teeth she was sinking nervously into her lower lip.

'Sometimes,' she managed, a sudden teasing smile curving her mouth.

Max smiled too. 'You begin to know me,' he drawled, half teasingly.

'Where are we going?'

'Get in and you'll find out.' He was still holding open the car door and Jassy obeyed, her body fluidly graceful as she slid into the low seat. A second later Max was beside her, his nearness overpowering in such small, close confines. The faint aroma of his after-shave filled her nostrils and a hard thigh touched hers briefly.

'Your stepfather gave his permission, I assume?' The softly spoken question jerked Jassy's head round, her eyes startled.

'Not exactly,' she replied with a frown.

'Meaning?' He was staring at her, dissecting her with green eyes as fierce as a tiger.

'I'd rather not talk about it.' She wished he had not mentioned Morgan, it was the last thing she wanted to think about.

'Tell me, Jassy,' Max ordered, tilting up her face and forcing her to look at him. He seemed to know that she could not lie to him.

'Why do you want to know?' she parried nervously.

'Tell me,' he repeated, ignoring her question and not letting her go.

'He was angry. He doesn't know I'm with you
now,' she said flatly, her eyes pleading with him to
drop the subject, her whole body trembling with the
fire of his touch.

Max frowned, a flash of anger darkening his face.

'When we get back, I'll come in with you—talk
to him.'

'No!' she cried, too quickly, jerking her head away
from his captive fingers, her eyes filling with tears.
'Don't spoil it, please,' she begged in a shaky little
voice.

Sighing, Max reached for her, pulling her into his
arms. Her tears were spilling out of her eyes and he
licked them away in a sensual intimate gesture, his
warm hard mouth moving over her face with hungry
tenderness.

'Oh, Jassy, I didn't mean to upset you,' he
murmured against her cheek. 'I want to help'

'I know, it's me, I'm just being silly.' She swallowed back her tears and took a deep breath, wishing
that she had the courage to put her mouth to his,
needing the healing warmth of his kiss. But she could
not find the courage, so instead she said, 'I'm starving—won't you tell me where we're going?'

Max released her, his face calm with understanding.

'Wait and see,' he replied with a smile, switching
on the engine.

Knowing that he would not push the subject of
Morgan any further, Jassy checked her make-up
briefly, then sat back, feeling a little more relaxed,
to enjoy the drive.

The restaurant was small and exclusive, and they
were shown to an intimate table by the owner, obviously a good friend of Max's.

Later, Jassy could not remember what she had
eaten. Sitting opposite Max, she was mesmerised by

his dark attractive face and burning green eyes, as they chatted over the meal. He was amusing and charming, gently coaxing away the last of her sadness, urging her to talk about herself unselfconsciously, and watching her, always watching her, as if he wanted to commit ever last detail of her to memory.

The wine gave her confidence and a brilliance to her eyes that captured Max's undivided attention. She was beautiful and intelligent and graceful, it came easily to her when she was with him. He made her feel totally feminine and aware of her need for a man.

As they left the restaurant some hours later, she swayed against him as the night air hit her, making her realise that although she was far from drunk, she had overdone it a little with the wine.

Max's mouth was gently indulgent as he led her to the car, his arm rock-hard as it coiled supportively around her slender shoulders.

She lay her head against his shoulder as they drove back, feeling totally happy and content. As they reached the hotel, he looked down at her flushed face and shining, jewel-bright eyes, with a brooding intensity.

His mouth touched hers briefly and she sensed that he was holding back, that he wanted more of her yielding lips.

She gazed up at the hard angles of his face. 'Thank you for a wonderful evening, and a lovely day,' she said with a bright smile.

'Thank you, Jassy—you made it perfect,' he murmured. Then with a groan of suppressed impatience, he reached for her again and kissed her fiercely, his mouth hard, hungry and demanding. Jassy read the glittering desire in his eyes with a responsive shiver of surrender, and they clung together urgently, uncaring of the discomfort in the small low car.

Then Max let her go, control stiffening his spine as he drew breath sharply and unevenly.

'I'll come in with you,' he said simply, his voice a little harsh.

'No, please, Max.' She had to face Morgan alone. 'You'd be the red rag to the bull. I have to sort it out myself, do you understand?' She was pleading with him anxiously.

Max sighed with frustration. 'As you wish.' It was obvious that he did not want to give up. He took a pen out of his jacket and scrawled something on a small white card. 'My number,' he said, handing it to her. 'If you need me, call—whatever time.'

Jassy took the card with a smile.

'Promise, Jassy,' he urged.

'I promise, and thank you for caring.' She leaned over and kissed his smooth, hard cheek.

'I do care, Jassy, remember that.'

His words rang in her ears as she slid out of the car, desperately trying to ignore the apprehension that was gripping her. Waving to Max, she walked towards the hotel entrance, feeling very much as though she was about to face a firing squad.

CHAPTER FIVE

MORGAN was waiting for her, his anger barely concealed as he paced backwards and forwards across the lounge.

Jassy closed the door behind her, swallowing convulsively, trepidation clawing in her stomach as she turned to face him.

Her stepfather's eyes slid over her, taking in the gypsy dress, the brilliance of her eyes and the bruised, thoroughly kissed quality of her mouth.

'Have you been with him?' he demanded, facing her across the room.

Jassy could feel the tentacles of his rage reaching for her, the whole room was filled with it.

'I've been with Max, yes,' she answered steadily and honestly.

Morgan swore violently. 'After what I told you before, you still defied me and went out with him?'

It was more of an angry statement than a question, and Jassy nodded. There was no need to answer. She had the terrible, fearful feeling that Morgan wanted to hit her. If she had been a man she felt sure that he would have punched her on the nose. She had never seen him so angry, but then she had never defied him before and he was not used to such behaviour.

'The moment my back's turned, you run to him like a lovesick child! It's going to stop, Jassy. You won't see him again, do you hear me?' he shouted, furiously.

Jassy took a deep, shaking breath. 'No, Morgan,

you've got no right to tell me who I can and cannot see. I like Max and I will see him again, if I choose to do so.' She had never gone against Morgan's wishes before, but the thought of never seeing Max again was too much to bear, galvanising her into action, into defiance. What she had feared ever since leaving school and coming to live with Morgan had finally happened. The independence and inner strength that boarding school had given her would not let Morgan rule her life for her. She was nineteen years old—old enough to make her own decisions and being used from an early age, to making such decisions alone, the very idea of letting somebody else take over was unthinkable and totally alien to her nature.

Perhaps she should have asserted herself before now, she thought miserably as she glanced at the dull red outrage on her stepfather's face. Perhaps if she had put her foot down over the clothes, the dinner invitations, little things like that, both of them would have been better prepared for this situation. But it was too late.

'You must understand, Morgan, that I have to choose who I see, my own friends.' She tried to explain to him, hoping that he would see reason, profoundly glad that she had not agreed to Max coming back with her. Morgan would have burst a blood vessel!

'You're engaged to René,' Morgan gritted through clenched teeth. 'And I'll make damned sure that you don't see Bellmer again. If he comes within a foot of this door, I'll personally knock his teeth down his throat—I'll kill him, is that clear?'

Jassy stared at him, hardly able to believe her ears. He had been oozing respectful politeness to Max only twenty-four hours ago and now he actively hated him. It was beyond understanding or belief. If it hadn't been so ugly, it would have been funny.

'I'm *not* engaged to René, that's something you've dreamed up yourself. I've told you time and time again that I have no intention of marrying him, because I don't love him. Don't you *ever* listen to me?' she retaliated angrily, her eyes flashing misery.

'Love?' Morgan scoffed openly. 'You have no conception of love!'

'I have,' Jassy cried, deeply hurt. 'I. . . .' she broke off just in time, horrified at the admission she had almost made. Did she love Max Bellmer? She had nearly told her stepfather just that.

'What have you got against Max anyway?' she asked desperately.

'You're too stupid to see that he's using you,' Morgan replied viciously.

'Using me? For what?' she asked incredulously, certain that she had nothing that Max could use.

'He's using you to get to me!' Morgan exploded, irritated beyond anger by the blank look Jassy gave him. 'He's been after this business for years. I've managed to hold him off, but it hasn't been easy. You're his ace,' said Morgan, bitter with rage.

Jassy shook her head disbelievingly. 'I don't believe you,' she said coldly. 'You see everybody's actions as connected with business. You just can't believe that some people don't give a damn about it. Max wouldn't do that anyway.' She was unshakeable in her belief in him.

Morgan gave a short ugly laugh. 'He won't get the chance,' he muttered grimly. 'I telephoned René when I got back to find you out—oh yes, it wasn't difficult to guess who you were with, where you were,' he said cruelly, his cold eyes raking her shocked, pale face. 'I've fixed the wedding date, exactly a month today!'

Jassy felt faint, the floor seemed to be moving beneath her feet, and the greedy triumph on her stepfather's face made her feel terribly ill inside. Had he gone mad? She stood shock-still, her whole body icy cold. This was some dreadful nightmare.

Please, God, let me wake up and find that it isn't true, she prayed in desperate silence, but the seconds ticked past and nothing changed.

'No . . . I won't do it,' she whispered, putting her hands up in front of her as if to ward off the physical blow of her stepfather's words.

'Yes, you will, Jassy, and if you see Bellmer again, René will find out, mark my words. He's got some pretty tough boys working for him—Bellmer will wish he'd never been born.' The semblance of a smile stretched Morgan's mouth as he spoke his soft threats.

It was the last straw, and Jassy could not bear it a second longer. She turned and fled from the room, her eyes blind and hysterical.

Morgan called her back impatiently, but she ignored him, flying like the wind down the stairs, her heart frozen with a kind of agony.

The smart young Spaniard on the reception desk stared at her curiously as she rushed past him, out of the doors and into the night. She could not see where she was going, it did not matter, as long as it was away from Morgan, her eyes misty with tears as the realisation of his true character sank in.

Moments later she collided stunningly into the hard unyielding body of a man, the contact knocking the breath from her lungs. Strong hands reached out and grasped her shoulders and she fought like a wildcat, imagining in her crazed state of mind that it was Morgan come to take her back to her room. He would probably lock her in until the wedding, she thought crazily, almost hysterical.

'Let me go!' she shouted, desperately struggling with all her might.

The hands on her shoulders shook her, rather roughly, into silence, into submission, and as she looked up through her tears, Max's face, dark with concern swam into vision.

'Jassy, what in hell's name is the matter?' he asked urgently. Morgan's threats came unbidden into her head. She could not bear Max to be harmed for her.

'Let me go,' she repeated. 'Please. It's not safe.' She was whispering as she tried to free herself, glancing wildly over her shoulder, expecting to see Morgan behind them at any second.

She managed to break free at a moment when Max's defences were down, and ran towards the beach, not listening to him and not waiting to see if he followed her.

I must get away, she kept repeating to herself over and over again.

She rushed across the road, barely missed by a motorbike, that swerved dangerously to avoid her, its rider shouting a tirade of abuse in Spanish.

Max caught up with her easily, seemingly without any effort at all, his hand closing on her arm and pulling her round to face him.

Jassy gazed at him mutely, noting the wildness and the anger in his darkly flashing eyes. It seemed inevitable that he was here and she did not question his presence or his anger.

'You crazy little fool!' he grated harshly, his fingers tightening cruelly on her bare arm. 'You nearly got yourself killed—Dear God, Jassy, you scared me, running into the road like that!' He seemed beyond control as he violently pulled her against his chest, crushing her shining head to his shoulder.

Jassy clung to him, revelling in his warmth and his comfort, her ear over the heavy, disturbed rhythm of his heart.

He held her with a tight desperation as if she was precious to him, his hand stroking back her hair. The tears that had blinded her were long gone now, and a cold heaviness had settled over her mind, leaving her numb and weary.

Finally Max held her away from him, not letting her go completely, his hands still resting lightly but firmly on her shoulders as though he feared that she would run from him again. He gazed down at her pale expressionless face, anger flaming dangerously in his green eyes, to see her so hurt.

'What happened?' he asked quietly, his voice tight with leashed fury and concern. But Jassy could only shake her head, unable to speak, putting a cold trembling hand over her face.

They were only yards away from the hotel. Morgan might be watching them from his window at this very moment. He would see her with Max and come down. Or he might phone René, she thought irrationally.

'Oh God, I have to get away from here, now. *Now*,' she whispered desperately. She reached up, her hands clenching on Max's jacket, tugging at the smooth material in anguish. 'Would you ... would you take me somewhere—anywhere, in your car ... please?' she begged, staring at him with eyes that were wild and bruised and very hurt.

'Of course,' Max answered immediately. 'You're safe now Jassy. No one will harm you, I promise,' he said gently, forcing her to listen to him, to take in the truth of his words.

'You don't understand. . . .' She was still trembling with shock and nervousness, and cursing savagely under his breath, Max slid his arm around her shoulders and led her to his car. Her legs felt very weak, so weak that she was surprised they were carrying her at all. She scrambled quickly into his car, glancing over her shoulder in blind apprehension.

Max watched every fearful, jerky movement she made with violent, intent eyes, as he switched on the engine and skidded the car on to the road with a screeching protest from the tyres.

He drove very fast along the coast road, his strong brown hands gripping the steering wheel so tightly that his knuckles gleamed white.

Jassy sat perfectly still beside him, staring straight ahead, her breathing shallow and barely noticeable.

Five minutes later the car jerked to a sudden halt on a deserted stretch of road. In front of them lay the ocean, the bright glint of the moon on the water, beautiful, but unnoticed by them both. Jassy, only just aware that the car had stopped, opened the door and got out, strolling down to the water's edge on still shaky legs, her arms wrapped around her body in a vulnerable, defensive gesture. Max watched her as she stood alone, staring with unseeing eyes over the dim ocean, then he too slid from the car and walked towards her.

She lifted her head as he approached, her face blank with shock and reaction.

'Thank you for bringing me here,' she said expressionlessly, her voice choking a little.

'Oh, Jassy!' He spoke her name with a soft, aching intensity, his perceptive eyes raking her forlorn face

and shivering body and narrowing with the wild
anger that he could barely control.

Jassy listened, his voice breaking into her conscious
mind, as she really saw him for the first time since
colliding with him outside her hotel. Feeling
strangely detached, she noted his air of barely-sup-
pressed impatience, the tightness of his mouth and
the terrible wildness in his eyes.

'Tell me, Jassy, for God's sake tell me!' he said
fiercely, standing so near that she could feel his cool
breath on her face and yet he was not touching her.
A question came into her eyes and he saw it, reading
her expression easily.

'What is it, child?' he muttered very gently.

'Will you hold me?' she whispered pleadingly.

The words had hardly left her lips when she was
lifted into his arms, her feet hardly touching the
ground, and he held her tightly, his mouth moving
against her soft hair. She did not move, but let him
hold her, he was so very strong and the warmth of
his body was gradually seeping through and melting the icyness of hers. How safe she felt, wrapped
so tightly within those rock-hard, muscled arms.
Surely nothing could touch her when she was with
Max.

She arched back her head, a graceful indication
that she was at last ready to talk, and he lowered
her, so that her feet were back on the ground, their
bodies moving against each other for one dizzying,
breathtaking moment. Looking down at her, he
smiled slightly in encouragement, although his eyes
were still filled with anger and concern.

'It's Morgan,' Jassy said very quietly, then
laughed a trifle hysterically. 'Who else?'

'He was angry with you for going out to dinner
with me?' Max questioned, his voice deadly.

Jassy nodded. 'Very angry, but it's worse than

that. . . .' She stopped, swallowing convulsively. 'He
. . . he said that if I saw you again, he'd . . . oh, it
doesn't matter. He's fixed the date of my wedding to
René,' she finished flatly.

Max drew a long, harsh breath. 'Without telling
you?'

'Yes—I've told him so many times that I won't
marry René, but he takes no notice. He can't care
for me if he's willing to force me into a loveless marriage, can he? I'm just a business asset to him,' she
said miserably, her eyes filling with tears again.

Max's arms tightened around her, offering comfort. 'He can't force you to marry against your
wishes,' he said in that same quiet, deadly voice.

'You don't know Morgan.' Jassy sniffed loudly,
managing a wan smile.

'Listen to me, Jassy, I mean it—he can't force
you.' His face was grim and she could feel the
powerful muscles of his body tightening with barely-
controlled anger.

'You don't understand,' she said sadly, feeling
defeated. 'Morgan manipulates people every day,
he's a master. Legally he can't force me to get
married, but there are other ways. He'll have a
thousand and one clever tactics up his sleeve, you
can bet.' Her voice was faintly bitter and Max
frowned heavily.

'I'll come back with you, and by God, I'll talk
some sense into him! Trust me.'

'No!' Jassy stared urgently into his face, her hand
tightening on his arm. 'You mustn't!'

'Why not? Tell me what else he said, Jassy.'

'He'll hurt you,' she said wildly, her fear alive in
her gentle brown eyes.

'I doubt it,' Max said coldly, and Jassy believed
him, but there was still René.

'It's not just Morgan, it's René—some of the men

who work for him, they're thugs. I remember things René used to tell me about Pierre, and how he used these men to frighten people who got in his way. . . .' Jassy had never believed these stories at the time, imagining that René was exaggerating, as he was prone to do. But Morgan's confirmation this evening that these men existed had thrown a new and sinister light on René's joking anecdotes.

A vision of Max, bleeding, hurt and unconscious, rose before her eyes, and she shuddered, almost crying out with the pain it brought in its wake.

'Please don't go, Max. Morgan will tell René . . . he said so . . . *please,*' she begged.

'Are you so concerned for my safety, dear Jassy?' Max asked softly, reaching out to touch her mouth with strong, gentle fingers. Meeting his eyes, Jassy saw that he was serious.

'Yes, I couldn't bear you to be hurt because of me,' she answered honestly, her lips trembling and cold as she spoke.

Max smiled, his green eyes warm and lazy as they rested on her pleading face.

'That's good to know,' he murmured, lowering his head to touch his firm mouth to her forehead in a brief caress. 'But I won't get hurt, honey—I've dealt with his sort before, and so help me, I'll kill him with my bare hands if he tries anything like that.' His voice was hard and suddenly violent, his teeth were clenched, tightening the stark bones of his face to a taut, frightening mask.

Jassy wondered at his concern for her. Perhaps he did care for her, she hoped so anyway. However, sweet thoughts like that would not help her in her present predicament. Even if she won, and did not have to marry René—which was doubtful, Morgan would make her life a living hell. There seemed no solution.

'Dear God, I have to get away from here,' she said desperately. 'Away from Morgan, at any rate.' She had wanted to veer the conversation away from the subject of Max coming back to the hotel with her, but she could see that his mind was made up.

'I wish you'd promise that you won't come back with me tonight,' she said slowly, glancing at him from beneath the thick fringe of her lashes.

'You know I won't do that,' Max said quietly. 'I can't let you go back alone.'

She sighed. The whole situation was fast spinning out of control. Morgan, René, Max, everything seemed to be closing in on her. Strange how forty-eight hours, such a short amount of time, could change a person's life, and turn a happy world upside down.

Max took her face between his hands, tilting it up to his. She stared into his hard, familiar face with fascination and a strange ache in her heart.

'I have a solution to all your problems,' he told her, his eyes glittering in the darkness as they fixed on her.

'What is it?' Jassy whispered, her heart beginning to pound with a slow languor. He was overpoweringly attractive, filling her senses with his nearness. Her hands moved against the unyielding hardness of his chest in restless exploration, totally unaware of her actions.

'You can marry me,' he said, so quietly that she thought she had misheard him.

She shook her head as if to dislodge a blockage in her ears.

'I'm sorry,' she giggled uncontrollably. 'I thought you said——'

'I did,' he cut in. 'I want you to marry me, Jassy.' He enunciated every word very clearly, his voice low and cool and gentle.

She froze for long moments as the impact of his words sank in. She had not dreamt that he would ask her. Could it be possible that he felt the same way as she did?

'You don't have to, you know,' she heard herself saying stupidly, a symptom of her shock.

'I realise that,' Max teased. And then his amusement was gone. 'God knows, I want to.' Jassy heard the naked, undisguised hunger in his voice, her whole body reacting to it.

'Max——' She whispered his name achingly as his mouth touched hers in a kiss so fierce that she involuntarily swayed her weight against him, uncertain that her legs would support her.

His lips parted hers expertly, hardening in deep passionate, demand at her trembling, inexperienced response. The hunger that she could feel inside him seemed to come from his very soul, as he gathered her against him possessively, his hands slowly sliding down the long smooth curve of her back, to hold her closer, if that was possible. Weakness was flooding her body, a warm ache that relaxed her helplessly in his arms.

Of their own volition Jassy's arms came around his neck, his hair thick and dark around her twining fingers. She stroked his neck and heard him draw breath sharply in response.

His mouth left the softness of her parted lips to trail its fire tenderly over her face, finding the sensitive hollow behind her ear. Jassy could not deny him as she let her head fall back, a soft moan escaping her.

Max lifted his head then, a fierce tenderness lighting his eyes as he gazed down at her, at her beautiful head still arched back, her golden hair wild and soft, glinting against the dark velvet of his jacket, at her closed eyes and invitingly parted lips. He drew a long breath and briefly kissed her small pointed chin.

'I want you, Jassy,' he muttered unevenly. 'And I always get what I want. You'll marry me?'

'Yes.' It was an immediate acceptance, a soft sigh as she surrendered to him. She opened her eyes and looked up at the magnificent hard-boned beauty of his face. She had lost her heart so easily, so completely. How could she care for him so much when she had only known him for two days? she asked herself wonderingly. He was heart-stoppingly attractive and he wanted her, but more than that she trusted him, felt safe with him. It was dangerous and naïve to harbour such feelings, she told herself sternly, because if there was one word that could *not* be used to describe Max Bellmer, it was 'safe'.

She would become his wife, and the thought brought with it a dizzying excitement so piercing that she could not think straight. Max was still staring down at her, his green eyes flame-bright with intensity, and a faint smile softening his mouth.

'You'll marry me as soon as possible—I've waited too damn long,' he asserted softly, putting her away from him with hands that shook a little and lighting two cigarettes, one of which he placed between her lips with a smile.

'Time to tell your stepfather,' he said firmly.

Jassy bit her lower lip, an unknown fear squeezing her heart.

'Max ... I ....' she began worriedly, feeling as though she ought to warn him about something, but not quite knowing what it was.

But Max silenced her, placing a finger over her lips.

'Don't worry, child, we'll go back now and tell him. There will be no problems, I promise you. You don't even need to stay there if you don't want to.'

'But where could I go?' she asked with a miserable shrug of her slim shoulders.

'You could stay with me,' he murmured softly and wickedly. 'Or you could stay with Roxanne and Tomás,' he added, openly amused by the shocked widening of her eyes at his first suggestion.

As they walked back to the car, Jassy thought about everything that had happened this evening. Her secret fear, a fear that had haunted her ever since leaving school, that Morgan did not care anything for her, had been proved horribly true. He had been very persistent that she lived with him after leaving school, and naïvely, she had not stopped to examine his motives. Without Morgan she would have been utterly alone in the world and he had been a last link with the mother she had loved so dearly.

Looking back, she realised that she had expected him to love her as his daughter. She knew now that it had been her worst mistake. He had used her ruthlessly, imagining that his wealth and the comfortable life he offered her were compensation enough.

Right from the beginning, he had assessed her potential, working out how she could serve him best. A good, profitable marriage—profitable from his point of view only, of course—was what he had been grooming her for, ever since the bright, lazy summer day, the last day of term, when he had arrived at the school, wreathed in affectionate smiles, to carry her away in his gleaming Bentley.

Even now Jassy could not blame him. It was in his nature, in his blood. Business was his way of life, love and affection—these words held no meaning for him, and perhaps Jassy had known it in her heart all along. Yes, it was her own fault, she thought ruefully, as Max pulled the car back on to the road and they sped towards her hotel. Throughout her adolescence Morgan had been a romantic figure in her life, taking the place of a father.

She had been much envied by her friends. Morgan Carrington was well-known, wealthy, successful and ruggedly handsome, but more than that, he was her stepfather, always arriving at the school with armfuls of expensive presents, taking her out and making her feel grown up. All these things had been balm to a love-starved teenager who had lost her mother.

She had clung to her illusions with vigour, and it was only as she had lived with him and begun to know what he was really like, that she had begun to fight. Right up to this evening she had stubbornly refused to believe that he really would force her to marry René against her wishes. How stupid could she be? she now asked herself scathingly.

Just before it was too late, the veils had been ripped from her eyes, and only a few hours before, as Morgan had ranted and raved at her, she had seen him clearly for the first time in her life and she had feared him. The callous manipulation that had governed her life for years had been revealed in all its shocking ugliness. She had fought for her very survival as a person in her own right and although she had won, for the moment at least, she had found herself back where she had been when her mother died, utterly alone in the world and unloved.

Magically, Max had saved her. She was not alone or unloved any longer. She had been drawn to him from the beginning, he had taken her over from that first moment of meeting. She had never believed in love at first sight, it had been the stuff of romantic fairytales, but now she knew it as fact. She had fallen in love with Max and fallen hard, from the moment she met him. It was useless to wonder how that could be, she could not explain it herself. Perhaps it was fate, her destiny to meet and fall in love with him.

He had asked her to marry him, offering her love and security for ever. It was like a dream. Dear God, how I love you, Max, she thought fiercely and silently, shocked by the depth of her feelings as she turned to look at his proud, stark profile in the darkness. I hope I can make you happy.

CHAPTER SIX

Four hours later, Jassy lay dry-eyed and incredibly wide awake in the darkness of a strange bedroom.

Roxanne and Tomás had discreetly not asked any questions when she and Max had arrived at the villa at such a late hour. It was obvious to them that something was wrong. Roxanne's worried glance had slid from Jassy, pale and tearful, her soft brown eyes blank and shocked, to Max, grim and violently angry, his powerful body tense and still, and she had offered help immediately.

She had tactfully left them alone in the huge lounge, with the excuse that she would get Jassy's room ready. As soon as she had gone Max had taken Jassy into his arms, stroking her cheek gently, and she had pressed her face to the hard warmth of his shoulder in desperate need.

'Are you okay?' he had asked, with such tenderness that she had felt bruised by it. She had felt deadly calm and had even managed a blank smile. She had grown up almost in a matter of minutes and the jolt into maturity had stunned her.

'Yes, I'm okay,' she had finally answered, unwilling for him to bear the pain and concern that shadowed his lean face, when he looked at her. 'But I feel exhausted.'

'I'd better leave then and let you get some sleep,' he had murmured reluctantly, obviously unwilling to leave her. He had kissed her briefly, his mouth warm and loving. 'I'll call round first thing in the morning,' he had promised. 'And if you need me tonight, call me, right?'

Then he had left the house, murmuring a few words to Roxanne on his way out. Jassy had sat perfectly still, listening to the roar of the car engine. He had gone, and she felt very lonely, regretting her white lie.

She had refused Roxanne's offer of coffee, thankful for the other woman's kindness. She had wanted to explain what had happened to Roxanne, her new friend, but somehow the words had not come and she had gone to bed soon after Max's departure.

She lay on her back now, very still, the effort of moving any part of her body too much for her, staring up at the ceiling.

The house was silent and dark, but her mind was buzzing with light and noise, and she could not sleep, the evening's events were spinning endlessly around in her head.

Max had taken her hand in his, squeezing it reassuringly as they had stepped into the lift that would take them up to Morgan. His bleak eyes had been raking her stricken face.

'There's nothing to worry about,' he had said with a thin smile. Jassy remembered wishing that she could believe him.

Max had flung open the door of the suite, without knocking, Jassy behind him, so physically frightened that her knees had been knocking together.

Morgan had been standing by the window, smoking, a brooding frown creasing his face. His cold eyes had flashed icy fury at the sight of Max.

Jassy closed her eyes, her head moving restlessly on the soft pillows as she thought about it now. The ugly scene that had ensued had been the most shocking thing in her life. The very sight of her and Max together had triggered off a terrible, bitter fury in Morgan that even now Jassy could not fully understand. As her stepfather had begun shouting,

Jassy had pulled free of Max, sinking down into one of the plush chairs, her hands pressed over her ears in a defensive effort to blot out what was being said.

Max had been ice cold, grim and frighteningly controlled, only the muscle jerking erratically in his jaw had given him away as being furiously angry.

He had won even before he started, because Morgan did not have a leg to stand on. Jassy was over eighteen, legally she could do as she pleased, and Morgan's threats had been completely dismissed by Max, as he destroyed the older man with a cold, ruthless precision that had frightened Jassy.

She had tried to intervene, but both men had ignored her. It had become a personal battle of wills between them and she had no part in it.

'Jassy is coming with me when I leave here tonight,' Max had said tersely. 'We are going to be married, with or without your consent. I don't give a damn about your consent, but I think Jassy would appreciate it.'

'You're going to wish you'd never defied me like this, I promise you!' Morgan had turned on Jassy, his voice threatening. She had shrunk fearfully farther into her seat.

'If you *ever* touch a hair on her head, I'll break you Carrington, and you know I can do it,' Max had cut in, in a dangerously soft voice, stopping Morgan dead in his tracks.

They had left the hotel soon afterwards. Jassy had collected her few most precious possessions, which she always carried with her, and Max had promised to collect the rest of her things for her later.

'You were very hard on him,' she had whispered to Max as they drove to Roxanne's villa. Max flashed her a dark glance, taking his eyes off the road for a second.

'Dammit, I had to be,' he had replied harshly. 'He

would have destroyed you, Jassy, don't you understand that?'

She had shrugged her slender shoulders in defeat, averting her eyes from his. 'So you destroyed him before he got the chance,' she had replied flatly, her voice totally devoid of expression.

Max's strong hands had clenched on the steering wheel, betraying his irritation with her. 'Do you think I enjoyed it?' he had asked grimly.

'How should I know?' she had replied uncaringly, too upset to be able to think straight.

'If that's what you want to think,' Max had said very coolly, making no excuses for his behaviour.

Jassy covered her face with shaking hands as she relived that short conversation, the release of tears finally forcing their way to the surface to wash away the intolerable pain she felt inside. She had made Max angry with her, practically blaming him for what had happened. How could she have been so unfair? she wondered now, as sobs racked her weary body. The long-term consequences of this evening were too painful to think about and, crying herself into exhaustion, she finally fell into a deep, dreamless sleep.

She was woken late the next morning by Roxanne bearing a cup of coffee with a worried expression. She shook Jassy's shoulder gently.

'Wake up, Jassy. I've brought you some coffee, and Max is here.'

Jassy struggled into wakefulness slowly, painfully aware as she forced open her eyes that her head was throbbing agonisingly. Roxanne pulled up the blinds and threw open the shutters and Jassy blinked in the bright light, a small gasp of pain escaping her.

'Headache?' Roxanne enquired sympathetically, surveying the pale beautiful girl in front of her.

'Yes, I feel dreadful,' Jassy replied ruefully.

'I'll get you some painkillers,' said Roxanne with a smile. 'And do you want any breakfast?'

'Oh no, I couldn't face food,' Jassy muttered with a heartfelt grimace.

Roxanne turned to leave the room. 'Max is pacing up and down like a caged lion out there. I'll tell him that he'll just have to wait,' she laughed.

'Thank you, Roxanne,' Jassy said quietly. 'Thank you for everything.'

Roxanne shrugged. 'You're welcome here,' she said lightly. 'And now—those tablets.'

She shut the door quietly and Jassy forced herself to sit up and sip the hot, delicious coffee. All the dreadful events of the previous day rushed back into her mind with a jolt as her head cleared and she became fully awake. It did not improve her headache.

The sky was an arch of pure bright blue outside the open window, the sweet, high call of the birds, noisy and insistent.

Jassy slid out of bed, feeling a little better for the coffee, although her head was still thumping with pain as she stood up. She walked to the window and looked out over the beach, finding the warm, faintly salted air, somehow soothing. The sun was high and she idly wondered what time it was. A knock on the door revealed Roxanne with the promised painkillers. Jassy swallowed them immediately, murmuring her thanks.

'Would it be possible for me to take a shower?' she asked Roxanne. She felt dreadfully hot and sticky.

'Of course. I was about to ask you if you wanted one.'

'Oh dear, I've just remembered that I didn't bring any clothes with me last night.' She looked around for the red gypsy dress. She would have to wear that.

'No problem,' Roxanne smiled, her eyes skimming over Jassy in quick calculation. 'I guess we're about the same size, I'll lend you something,' she said brightly. It was a great relief. Jassy did not think that she would ever be able to wear her red dress again in comfort. It would always remind her.

'That's great, thanks. By the way what time is it?'

Roxanne consulted the small gold watch on her wrist. 'Just before one.'

'Good heavens! How could I have slept so late?' Jassy asked, appalled.

'I didn't have the heart to wake you before,' Roxanne said laughingly.

'What time did Max get here?' Her face flushed a little as she spoke his name.

'About nine-thirty. He looks dreadful—I don't think he got any sleep last night. You'll see for yourself anyway.'

She led Jassy to the shower and left her to it, while she went in search of some suitable clothes. Jassy stepped out of her underwear into the elegant dark-blue tiled shower and turned the taps full on, the pelting cold water making her gasp. She washed her hair, lingering under the cool jets of refreshing water, and on stepping out and winding a huge fluffy towel around herself, sarong-wise, she found a neat pile of clothes waiting for her.

Smiling and feeling very much better, her head-ache practically gone, she dried herself quickly and slipped on the pale green cotton skirt and matching tee-shirt that Roxanne had lent her. They fitted perfectly.

Clever, kind Roxanne, she thought affectionately, as she brushed out her hair and tied it in a ponytail. She had not brought any make-up with her, in her flight from the hotel, and not wanting to impose on Roxanne more than she had to, she left her face bare. I look like a schoolgirl, she thought wryly, glancing at her face in the mirror. Too bad.

It was time to face Max, so taking a deep trembling breath, she left the bathroom, her bare white feet making no sound on the cool marble floors as she went in search of him.

He was alone in the lounge, standing by the window, gazing out at the ocean, his back to her, his powerful shoulders hunched. She watched him silently for a moment, a warm tide of fierce emotion washing over her at the sight of him.

'Max. . . .' She spoke his name softly and he spun round to face her, his inscrutable green eyes travelling slowly over her, devouring her damp shining hair, the pure young beauty of her face and the tense slenderness of her body, in the bright borrowed clothes. And all this time, she was watching him. His lean face looked haggard, lines of tiredness and strain tightening his mouth. He wore faded jeans and a dark open-necked shirt, his aggressive sexual aura weakening her legs.

She walked slowly towards him, unaware of her own soothing grace, but totally aware of his intent eyes, stopping right in front of him.

'You look tired,' she said gently, reaching up and touching the hard bones of his face, her soft eyes brilliant, in the stark light that flooded the room.

'Oh, Jassy,' he groaned softly, ignoring her remark, still staring down at her with devouring eyes. He swung her into his arms, his hand tilting her small face to receive his deep, hungry kiss.

She clung to him, returning that kiss with a passion that she had not known existed inside herself, her arms tight around his neck as she recognised his fierce need and her own longing to assuage it.

'I've been waiting for you,' he said simply, not letting her go.

'I know, Roxanne told me,' Jassy replied, her eyes drowsy as she looked at him.

He buried his face against her neck, breathing deeply. 'You smell beautiful,' he muttered softly, laughing deep in his throat at her shivering response.

She pushed at his wide shoulders, laughter bubbling inside her.

'Where are Roxanne and Tomás?' she asked curiously. The house seemed empty.

'They've taken Rafael and gone out, to leave us alone together,' Max explained, with a wicked glint in his eye.

'They're so kind,' Jassy sighed, wishing that there was some way she could repay them for all they had done.

Max nodded, reaching into the pocket of his shirt and pulling out a small black box. He handed it to her.

'What is it? Is it for me?' she asked excitedly.

'Open it and see.' His eyes rested indulgently on her as she examined the small box. It bore, in gold letters, the name and address of a famous New York jewellers, obviously very exclusive. She flipped back the lid, gasping at what lay inside, nestling against dark velvet. It was a diamond engagement ring, one huge flawless stone set in a simple band of gold.

Her eyes filled with tears of pure happiness, the diamond dissolving into a thousand rainbow pieces as she looked at it. Max took the ring from her trembling fingers and slipped it on to her wedding finger. It fitted perfectly.

'You're very quiet, don't you like it?' he teased her gently. Jassy stared down at her hand, the ring felt strangely cool and beautiful against her skin, a mark of his possession.

'It's beautiful,' she whispered. 'Quite beautiful.' She lifted her golden head to kiss him, moving her lips shyly against his mouth, until his arms tightened around her and she was carried away on the tide of his fierce desire.

Finally, reluctantly, he let her go, staring down at her with dark, disturbing eyes, his breathing forced and shallow.

'There's a lot to talk about, a lot to be planned,' he said unevenly, lighting a cigarette with practised ease and offering her one which she refused. He drew deeply on the cigarette.

'I'm too old for you, Jassy,' he said suddenly. 'Too goddamned old! If you ever. . . .'

She stopped him mid-word, closing his mouth with her own in a brief kiss.

'No, don't talk like that. You're not too old for me—how could you be?' she asked wonderingly. Then a remembered question popped into her mind. 'Last night, when I collided with you outside the hotel, why were you there?'

Max smiled. 'I was coming to see you. After you'd gone I realised that I couldn't leave you alone with him,' he admitted wryly.

'Oh, I see.' Jassy digested this with a warm glow around her heart. 'I was unfair to you last night, the things I said about the way you treated Morgan. I'm sorry, I didn't mean any of them.' She was anxious to apologise, because her unjust words had been preying on her mind.

'You were upset—it doesn't matter,' Max said gently, kissing her sad mouth thoroughly.

They spent the afternoon making plans. Max prepared a late lunch for them both, of cold meat and cheese and crusty bread, washed down with wine and followed by fresh fruit.

They ate outdoors, both hungry, talking all the

while. Max intended to get a special licence and they would be married in London as soon as possible.

Jassy's head was whirling as everything was sorted out, precisely and quickly, by Max. Until they flew back to London, Jassy would stay with Roxanne and Tomás.

Late in the afternoon, they went for a swim, lazily happy to be together, and when Roxanne and Tomás returned for dinner, Max told them of the forthcoming wedding. They were thrilled.

'I'm so very happy for you both,' Roxanne said huskily. 'I knew you were the one, Jassy, when he first talked of you. Max has waited a long time for the right woman, I'm glad it's you.'

Jassy felt deeply touched by Roxanne's words. 'Thank you, and I can't imagine a nicer sister-in-law than you,' she answered sincerely.

Dinner was a celebration. Tomás produced champagne and Jassy and Roxanne prepared a special meal which they ate in the open air, by candlelight. By the time Max left it was very late, and Jassy was sleepy and a little intoxicated with all the champage she had drunk.

Max held her in his arms, his green eyes dark and regretful as they parted, and kissed her with hungry tenderness, his warm sensual mouth playing havoc with her senses. Then he was gone and Jassy went to bed, drifting easily into sleep, happier than she had ever been in her life.

Max had business to attend to the following day and Jassy arranged to meet him for dinner. Roxanne was going into the city and asked Jassy to go with her. Jassy agreed readily, it would give her a good opportunity to do some shopping for her wedding.

When her mother had died, she had left Jassy some money, quite a sizeable amount which Jassy had been saving for just such an occasion. She intended using it now, to buy everything she needed, the only problem being that the money was in her London bank account. Roxanne once again came to the rescue.

'I have an account here, and I can lend you the money,' she said, as soon as she heard Jassy's problem.

'Would you? I can give you a cheque now,' Jassy said excitedly, pleased with such luck, and such kindness.

Roxanne was not worried about the cheque, so Jassy had to insist. They drove down the coast to the city in Roxanne's small car, with Jassy sitting in the back holding a sleepy Rafael. Roxanne did not believe in having a nanny for her child—probably, as she explained, because she and Max had never had a mother of their own, and Jassy agreed.

Jassy looked at the tiny child in her arms with wonder. Perhaps one day she would have a child like Rafael, Max's child. Small and dark, with those remarkable green eyes—the very thought was so beautiful that it was almost painful.

Parking the car, they decided to go for coffee before starting their shopping. The small restaurant that Roxanne chose was in a large square, lush with palm trees and brilliant tropical vegetation. The outdoor tables were shaded with bright parasols and Jassy looked around with curiosity as Roxanne ordered two coffees and milk for Rafael, her interest caught by the small kiosks around the edge of the square that were filled with bright postcards and local craftwork. Their coffee arrived almost immediately, the dark young waiter murmuring something in Spanish to Jassy. She did not understand what he said, so smiled at him blandly.

'He was admiring your hair,' Roxanne said wryly,

as they were left alone. Jassy shrugged, uncaringly, and glanced down into the fold-up pram beside Roxanne. Rafael was gurgling happily, his tiny brown feet kicking in the air.

'You're so lucky, Roxanne,' she said enviously. 'Rafael is the most beautiful baby I've ever seen.'

'You won't think that when you have your own,' Roxanne laughed, wisely. 'He's not all beauty, I can assure you. Sometimes he's the devil himself!' Her face was tender, though, as she lifted the baby from the pram and gave him his milk.

'How long have you been married?' Jassy asked, watching the other woman's gentleness with her child, her heart melting.

'Three years. I met Tomás at a party Max threw in New York, it was love at first sight.' Her face was dreamy with reminiscence. 'He was so different from any of the men I'd met before, so charming and gallant. American men are definitely lacking in that quarter!' she finished with a laugh.

'Except Max,' Jassy added.

'Max is an exception, and let's face it, we're both prejudiced.' They smiled at each other over their coffee cups.

'I'm going to see Morgan—that's my stepfather—this afternoon,' Jassy suddenly confided, her face sobering.

'Do you think that's wise?' Roxanne asked quietly, her face concerned.

Jassy frowned. 'I don't know, but I feel I have to see him again—just one last time, if that's what he wants, to try and explain why I couldn't marry René.' She sighed at the enormity of this task, and Roxanne squeezed her arm comfortingly.

'Shall I come with you?'

'Thanks for offering, but no.' All at once, Jassy wanted to confide in Roxanne, to tell her everything.

'Did Max tell you about the row with Morgan?'
Roxanne shook her head. 'It was dreadful.' Even
now the thought of it made Jassy shudder, as she
briefly explained the events leading up to it. 'I've
known him all my life, you see, and in his own way,
I think he has tried to be a father to me. That's why
I feel I must see him,' she finished, pleading for the
other woman's understanding.

Roxanne gave a low, unladylike whistle of pure
astonishment.

'I think we need some more coffee,' she said firmly,
attracting the waiter's attention and ordering some.

Staring at Jassy, she asked, 'Would he really have
forced you into this marriage?'

Jassy lowered her head. 'I thought not, until the
day before yesterday. He was pushing for it, of
course, I knew that. We'd argued about it many
times. He'd make little plans to push us together,
like inviting Pierre and René for dinner, then leaving
us alone while he and Pierre talked business, that
sort of thing.'

'You don't feel anything for René?' Roxanne
asked.

'I liked him,' Jassy replied honestly. 'I thought we
were two of a kind, but since we've been here, he's
made it clear that he would be in favour of the marriage—which came as a shock—we'd always joked
about it before. And I've seen a sullen, hard side to
him that I never saw before,' she sighed. 'It would
seem as though I've been living in a dream world all
my life. Morgan, René—how could I have been so
wrong?'

'We all make mistakes about people, Jassy,
especially those close to us. Sometimes it takes a by-
stander, a person from outside the circle, to put
things into perspective,' Roxanne said gently.

'Max?' Jassy smiled.

'Right. I understand how you feel about your stepfather. It would be impossible for you to cut him out of your life without a backward glance, whatever he's done.' Roxanne was very sweet and sympathetic.

'The trouble is that I feel as though I'm going to see a stranger, a Morgan I don't know at all. Oh what a mess! I'm so sorry for dragging you and Tomás into it all. I'm glad we're going to be friends, though,' she added sincerely.

'I'm glad too. I always prayed that I would be friends with Max's wife, and now my prayers are answered,' Roxanne said seriously. 'We'd better make a start on this shopping, or we'll never be through!'

After lunch, Roxanne dropped Jassy off at Morgan's hotel, on her way back to the villa.

The morning's shopping had been extremely successful and Jassy had acquired a complete new wardrobe—her trousseau, Roxanne had sternly informed her. She had also bought a present for Max, a black silk dressing gown, and a gold necklace for Roxanne.

She had known, the moment she saw the dressing gown, that it was for Max. The shop assistant had wrapped it elegantly for her, as Jassy had wondered when she would give it to him.

It had occurred to her then that she had no idea when his birthday was. This lack of knowledge had triggered off a strange sensation of panic as she had counted out the money from her purse, for the gift. I know nothing about him, and yet I'm going to marry him next week, she had thought frantically.

But at that moment Roxanne had diverted her attention and her fear had passed. As she stood outside the hotel, now, trying to pluck up the courage to go in, she remembered that moment of blind panic, and it halted her for a second. I love Max, she told herself desperately, bringing to mind his lean face and the desire she always felt in his arms, the fierce emotion he always aroused in her. Yes, I love him, time doesn't matter. I'll soon find out all the small details about him.

Reassured, she walked through the foyer of the hotel to the lifts. She had considered telephoning before arriving, but something inside her had held back. She would go straight to her stepfather's suite and ask if he would see her.

She did not want to give him time to brood, to think up any of his clever schemes. Please God, don't let René or Pierre be here, she thought, crossing her fingers as she reached the door and knocked tentatively. No answer. Just my luck to call when he's out, she thought irritably, her nerves feeling as taut as violin strings.

She knocked again, louder. 'Come in,' Morgan barked from within.

He sounded annoyed, but it was too late to back out now, so with legs that trembled violently Jassy opened the door and walked inside.

Morgan was sitting at the desk, a cigar smouldering in the ashtray at his side, as he leafed through a thick sheaf of papers. He did not look up.

'Hello, Morgan, can I come in?' she asked quietly, her heart beating so loud that she felt sure he would hear it, and she would give herself away. On no account would she let him see how he intimidated her. That was his strength, and she had no intention of handing herself to him on a plate, to be bullied into submission.

He looked up slowly, his light eyes skimming over her without warmth.

'So,' he said arrogantly, 'you've come to your senses at last.'

Jassy sighed. This was not going to be easy, although she had never imagined it would be.

'Can we talk?' she asked, ignoring his ridiculous remark.

'There's nothing to talk about. Your room is as you left it. You can arrange dinner with René tonight, and ask him to forgive you for. . . .'

'Morgan, please! I'm not coming back here. I came . . . I came to try and improve things between us,' she said beseechingly, trying to quell the faint prickle of anger that his words had aroused. Ask René to forgive her, indeed! She had done nothing wrong. If he and her stepfather had jumped to all sorts of conclusions, then that was hardly her fault.

Morgan was staring at her as though she had gone stark, staring mad.

'If you don't intend coming back here, or marrying René, how the hell do you expect to improve things between us?' he asked, cruelly mimicking her words.

'I don't love René. Surely you wouldn't force me into a loveless marriage?' Jassy cried, stung.

Morgan shrugged uncaringly. 'Force? Loveless marriage? You talk like an empty-headed schoolgirl,' he said coldly. 'René would make you a good husband.'

'Good for you maybe, but not for me,' Jassy cut in heatedly, only just keeping a rein on her temper.

They were at each other's throats already, and there seemed no hope of reconciliation. She could not understand Morgan's attitude at all. Was this terrible anger because she had defied him, or did it have something to do with Max, or René? It was totally beyond her.

She had to make one last effort. Taking a deep breath, she said,

'Please try to understand, Morgan. I love Max

and I'm going to marry him. I care for you too and I can't bear this bitterness. I can't marry René, even for you, it would be immoral, you must see that.' Oh dear, she thought, I'm making a terrible mess of this. I should have planned what I was going to say beforehand. It was so unnerving, though. She glanced apprehensively at her stepfather. A dull red anger suffused his face. He was furious.

'I see no such thing,' he snapped. 'What I do see is an ungrateful little bitch. I fed you, clothed you, took you in and gave you the sort of life that most girls your age would give their right arm for. I gave you everything and this is how you repay me. Presumably, you're still too damned naïve to see the true reason behind Bellmer's proposal, but if you think I'm going to sit back without a fight, you're mistaken. I'll make life difficult for you, Jassy, and when you fall flat on your face, don't expect me to pick you up!'

'Morgan . . . please. . . .' Her eyes pleaded with him, terribly hurt, but he did not even look at her.

'Collect your things.' He indicated the bedroom with a dismissive wave of his hand. 'And go. I never want to see you again, is that clear?'

CHAPTER SEVEN

A week later in England, Jassy sat beside Max in his car as it sped out of the London traffic towards the country and his home.

She relaxed against the plush black leather, feeling numb and very cold. They had not spoken since leaving the small wedding reception and she glanced covertly at the man beside her, a tremor running through her as she did so. Formal and remote in the expensively-cut dark suit he had worn for the ceremony, he was a stranger to her, a powerful, beautiful, frightening stranger, and she felt dizzy to think that she was his wife.

The heavy gold band on her finger seemed to weigh a ton and she twisted it nervously, as if trying to remove it.

Max caught her jerky actions in the corner of his eye, turning to flash her an inscrutable look from beneath heavy eyelids. His mouth twisted.

'Too late for second thoughts,' he said expressionlessly, as if he sensed that something was wrong, his voice shivering down her spine.

She did not answer, turning her face away to stare out of the window. How very true, she thought bitterly, consciously keeping her hands still, not wanting to attract his attention in any way.

She had been so happy until this morning. The past week had flashed by in a whirl of breathless preparations, and there had not been a moment to think about what she was going to do. Oh no, Max had given her no time for doubts, she thought wearily, unable to stop herself shifting restlessly in the soft seat, her gentle brown eyes moving blindly over the expensive interior of the black Mercedes.

There had been so much to do, the flight back to England to be arranged, plans for the wedding, shopping expeditions and Max had been with her all the time, taking over her life, arranging everything. They had dinner together every evening. Jassy had sat opposite to him, sipping the wine that eased her inner turmoil, mesmerised by the green glitter of his eyes, until nothing had mattered except being with him.

By asking casual questions and urging her to talk, he had let her reveal everything about herself, she had unselfconsciously opened her life to him, letting him know her intimately, until he knew her as well as she knew herself, and there were no secrets that she had not told him.

She realised now that, although he knew all about her, she had learned hardly anything about him. After her panic when buying the dressing gown, which she had still not given to him, she had asked him about himself, but it came to her now that he had been very guarded, not giving much away, with such charm that she had hardly noticed.

All she knew was that he was dangerously attractive, shrewd and intelligent, ruthless in pursuit of what he wanted and terribly wealthy. Hardly enough to base a lifelong commitment on. But still she had never doubted him for a second, she thought wildly, until this morning.

She had been eating her breakfast, feeling nervous and excited, when the knock had come on the door of her suite. Still sipping her coffee, she had wandered over to open the door, expecting it to be Roxanne, who had promised to help her get ready.

'You're early. . . .' she began, the words catching in her throat as she saw who stood outside. It was René.

'Can I come in, Jassy?' he asked politely, his eyes appraising as they slid over her damp hair and the clinging silk wrap she had thrown on after her shower.

'What are you doing here?' she asked incredulously, still shocked by his appearance in London.

'I wish to talk to you. Can I come in?' he repeated calmly.

Jassy stared at him. He looked pale and tired and very young. 'Very well. But you can't stay long. I'm getting married this morning, and I haven't much time.'

René's mouth tightened at her words, but he remained silent as he stepped into the room.

'Very pleasant,' he remarked, looking around as though he had all the time in the world.

'Yes,' Jassy agreed, wishing that he would say what he had come to say, then go.

She had been staying in this hotel suite since arriving in London. She had turned down Max's offer of staying in his house while he stayed with friends. It had seemed wrong. When she went to live in his house, she wanted it to be as his wife. She had also turned down Roxanne's offer of accommodation, wanting to stay in the city. Roxanne and Tomás lived well outside of London, when in England, in the country. Staying in London meant that she could see to last-minute preparations and get in touch with her friends. She also felt, privately, that Roxanne and Tomás had been put out enough, on her account.

So Max had arranged this suite for her, teasing her indulgently about her superstition. It was very pleasant, the views from the windows panoramic, situated as it was on the top floor of a well-known and exclusive hotel.

However, she did not feel inclined to discuss its merits with René so early on her wedding morning.

'What do you want to talk about?' she asked suspiciously, when it became clear after several seconds' silence that René was not going to make the first move. She wondered if Morgan had sent him. It would not surprise her.

'I want you to call off this wedding and marry me.' He said it so calmly and so casually that it did not sink in for a second.

'Don't be silly, René. I want to marry Max,' she said lightly, doubting his seriousness and hoping to keep their conversation brief and fairly friendly.

But it was not to be. René's mouth thinned angrily. 'You hardly know him,' he said coldly. 'You cannot possibly know whether or not you wish to marry him.' Jassy felt a spark of irritation at his sullen arrogance.

'I know him well enough,' she answered in a equally cool voice. 'But it's really none of your business, and I think you'd better leave.'

How dared he come to her on her wedding day and try to fill her mind with doubts?

'I'm not leaving until you see sense and change your mind,' René replied haughtily.

'What is this?' Jassy laughed, unable to believe his pompous behaviour. 'Did Morgan send you?'

'Your disrespect for your stepfather does not do you credit,' René said angrily, not answering her question.

Jassy was incensed. 'How dare you . . .?' she began furiously.

'I dare, because I intend you to marry me, not Bellmer,' René cut in icily. 'How much do you know about him? Not enough, I'm sure.'

'Get out of here! I won't listen to you,' Jassy choked, feeling sick and miserable, and sure that Morgan was behind all this. René seemed like a ventriloquist's dummy mouthing her stepfather's words. René gave a thin angry smile and strolled over towards the window.

'Do you know, for instance, that Bellmer has been after your stepfather's company for years, without success?' He glanced at Jassy's pale face. 'I can see that you don't. You are not stupid, Jassy, you can surely see your own part in his plans. . . .'

'You're a liar, René, you're like Morgan. Don't think I can't see through you. Please leave,' Jassy whispered, sickened by his cruelty, his tenacity.

'It seems that I may have been mistaken. Perhaps you are a fool, too naïve to see how Bellmer is manipulating you. When he finally gets his hands on your shares, just remember, it will be you who has destroyed your stepfather. I hope that will please you.' He turned from the window in a sharp ugly movement and began to walk towards the door.

'Shares?' Jassy whispered. 'What shares?' She was staring at him, her eyes dull, her face deathly white, a ghastly feeling of impending doom holding her in its grip.

'This is hardly the time for games,' René snapped. Then as he saw her stricken face, he laughed out loud. 'You really don't know? My God, Morgan plays it close to his chest!' He laughed again.

'Tell me,' Jassy urged, hardly able to bear his hostile amusement.

He looked at her consideringly, toying with her. 'I think I will, *chérie*. It's time you knew.' He paused, as if for effect, before continuing. 'When your mother married your stepfather he gave her, as a wedding present, fifty per cent of the company shares. God knows why, it was a damned fool thing to do, and he's paying for his loving gesture now. So, when your mother died, it was discovered that she had left the shares, not to your stepfather, but to you, in her will. Morgan has control of them until you are twenty-one, then they will become yours, to do with as you will. Your stepfather has had every legal brain in the country trying to break that will. It cannot be done.' He shrugged cynically. 'Your mother was a very clever woman.'

Jassy's legs would not hold her up and she sank into a chair, knocking her coffee cup off the table and not noticing.

Suddenly everything was clear—Morgan's hatred for Max, his fury that they were to be married. It was all too much to cope with, at once, and she covered her face with trembling hands, unaware of René's cold, detached eyes upon her.

What hurt most was the fact that Morgan had not told her about the shares. He would have forced her to marry René, without compunction, to keep hold of those shares—no doubt they had an agreement between them. It was horrible!

'I didn't know. . . .' she whispered, almost to herself.

René was at the door, about to leave, his work done.

'Bellmer did,' he said very clearly. 'He only has to wait two years and the company will fall into his hands. Remember that when you are in his bed, Jassy.'

She flinched from the savage blow of his words. It was his parting shot and he left the suite quietly, his cold, thin, triumphant smile chilling the air around her, and she was alone.

She did not move. She sat perfectly still, her body

trembling violently. She felt very confused, her mind whirling around in circles. She did not give a damn about the shares, only the effect they had on the people around her. She could almost understand René. He had wanted her and he had wanted the shares, she thought bitterly, and she had turned him down flat, wounding his massive pride. She would not forget his bitter cruelty, though, not ever. He had acted unforgivably.

She got to her feet shakily, desperately wanting to cry and finding herself unable to, she felt too numb and cold inside. Max knew about the shares. Was that why he wanted her? No, she could not accept that or she would go mad. Every part of her screamed against it. Will nobody ever want me for myself? she asked herself sadly. Every man in the world seemed at that moment to be hard and ruthless, with an unfeeling desire to manipulate people for personal gain. She could trust none of them.

Her fear of being used, yet again, coupled with a deep-rooted lack of self-confidence, filled her with sudden doubts about her marriage to Max. She had been amazed that he wanted her, and he had seemed so very different from all the other men she had ever met. What a fool she had been! Now she knew the truth. He was exactly the same as Morgan and René and Pierre and all the others.

Naïve and stupid. Both Morgan and René had called her those things, and they had been right. She loved Max, even now she loved him, and that was the most bitter blow of all.

Then it struck her. He had never mentioned love. Not once. She thought back to all the time they had spent together, raking through their conversations for a ray of hope, that she could not find. He wanted her, but he did not love her. A cold hand seemed to be squeezing her heart so painfully that she thought she might die. It can't be true, she told herself again and again, but a tiny nagging voice in her head told her that it had surely been proved beyond doubt. She had fallen hopelessly in love with a man who saw her only as a means to an end.

She would not marry him. That would thwart his plans, she thought wildly, the terrible pain inside her, demanding revenge for what he had done to her. But then her head began to clear. If she did not marry Max, what would she do? She could not go back to Morgan, although he would hear that she had not married Max, and no doubt rejoice. He would know that she had 'fallen flat on her face', as he had so charmingly put it, and Jassy suddenly found that unacceptable to her already shaky pride. She might have fallen out of the frying pan into the fire, so to speak, but her stepfather and René would never know.

Her decision was suddenly made. She would marry Max and have her revenge on him. She was finished with people using her and she would make him suffer for trying. She would not let him touch her, ever, and furthermore, she would not let him touch the shares when they legally came under her control. She would sign them over to Morgan, after all, they were the only thing he cared about. One of them at least would be happy, she mused bitterly, her anger and emotional turmoil unbalancing her thinking a little.

By the time Roxanne arrived, Jassy was composed, if a little pale. Her quietness was mistaken by Roxanne for bridal nerves, the other woman totally unaware of the misery that lay like a hard stone in Jassy's heart.

The ceremony was simple and quiet. Jassy looked quite breathtaking in a white silk dress that she had chosen with Roxanne's help. It clung to her high breasts and narrow waist, falling in soft folds over her slender hips to just below her knees. Her golden hair was coiled on the top of her head, threaded with tiny white flowers, soft tendrils caressing her cheeks and the vulnerable nape of her neck. She wore diamond teardrop earrings, a present from Roxanne and Tomás that shimmered against the creamy paleness of her skin, and carried a small bouquet of white, beautifully-fragrant freesias, her favourite flowers.

As she walked towards Max, she heard the sudden hiss of his indrawn breath, with a pang of self-doubt at what she intended to do. He watched her intently as she moved gracefully to his side, the purity and the innocent beauty of her, tearing at his heart.

Jassy glanced up at him, her heart thumping heavily as she looked briefly into his fierce, unreadable green eyes. His hair was carefully groomed, his dark suit perfectly cut to his powerful body. He seemed very remote, but the potent force of his devastating personality held her helplessly at his side when she wanted to run for her life from the register office.

The words of the marriage ceremony, huskily spoken by Max, were almost her undoing, and her hand trembled violently as he slipped the heavy band of gold that stated his ownership so positively on to her finger. Then, to her relief, the ceremony was over and he was tilting her face to receive his kiss, his mouth warm and sensual against her cold, stiff and unresponsive lips.

His lazy eyes sharpened on her pale face as she pulled away nervously, but he said nothing, merely taking her arm as they left the building.

The wedding breakfast that followed was a small,

select affair, with only the people who had attended the ceremony. Jassy had pleaded for this when the plans were being made. There was to be a larger, more formal reception in a month's time, when she was to be introduced to all Max's friends and associates.

She had also revealed some unorthodox plans for the honeymoon, which Max had agreed to. He had told her about his house in the country and she had longed to see it, begging him to let them spend some time there before going away on their honeymoon. Max had been indulgent, wishing her to be happy, aware of her youth and her nervousness, so now they were driving to his house in silence.

It was all so different from how she had imagined it. She had wanted to be alone with him after the ceremony, but now she cursed the wish that had thrown her into this isolated situation. They would be alone, just the two of them, deep in the English countryside.

A small sigh escaped her as desolation washed over her. Her life was in such a mess. Two weeks before, everything had been fine, she had been oblivious to the undercurrents in her life, but now. . . .

Able to think straight, she regretted the wild madness that had sent her to the register office with revenge in her mind. 'Too late for second thoughts,' Max's words echoed in her head. If only I didn't love him, she thought achingly.

'Why so quiet, Jassy?' Max's voice cut into her reverie. 'You haven't said a word since we left the party.'

'I'm tired,' she said stiffly, trying to sound normal and not quite succeeding.

'Rest if you like, I'll wake you when we get there,' he said gently, his voice very deep. 'You can use my shoulder.'

The thought of any physical contact with him made her senses reel and she shrank back further into her seat.

'No ... no, I'll be fine here,' she replied a little too quickly.

'As you wish.' His voice was impassive, but his dark brows met in a frown, as he cast her a probing look.

Jassy turned away to look out of the window again, deeply aware of him next to her. He was so near that she could hear him breathing if she listened hard. His hands resting lightly on the steering wheel were strong and long-fingered, and the vivid memory of their caress on her body filled her with a sweet, aching weakness. It came as a shock, with the knowledge that he did not love her, to find that she still wanted him. She closed her eyes tightly, trying to force such treacherous thoughts out of her head.

'If you're not going to sleep, would you light me a cigarette?'

She jumped, startled by his voice.

'Yes, of course,' she replied, extracting two from the packet in front of her. She lit one, and leaning over placed it between his lips, making sure that there was no contact, then quickly withdrew to her own corner of the car, to smoke the other one.

Max noted her actions with a slight tightening of his mouth, expelling smoke from his nostrils in a long, sharp stream. Sensing how withdrawn she was, he lapsed into silence for the rest of the journey.

Finally, the sleek black car pulled off the road, through high wrought-iron gates, wild with rhododendrons, and along a gravelled drive. Jassy sat up in her seat, her attention caught by smooth rolling lawns, dotted with trees, and flowers, a rioting profusion of flowers.

As they turned a corner, the house came into view and despite herself, she gasped, staring at it with wonder. It was the most beautiful house she had ever seen, mellowed stone, sheltered and surrounded by trees and covered with ivy, its windows glinting in the afternoon sun.

The car slid to a silent halt outside the front door, a huge wooden arch, surrounded by baskets of hanging flowers, their perfume scenting the warm air, their colours dazzling the eye. Max was watching her carefully, reading her rapt face.

'It's beautiful,' she whispered, forgetting everything else.

'I'm glad you think so,' he said with a faint smile.

He got out of the car and strolled round to open the door for her. Ignoring the hand he held out to her, and avoiding the sudden glint she saw in his green eyes, she slid out of the car, her high-heeled shoes crunching noisily on the gravel. She stood in front of the door, gazing up at a small arched window above. Stained glass letters spelled out the word OAKDENE.

Oakdene, she said it to herself, and it sounded good, rolling easily off her tongue.

Max was standing behind her, watching her with narrowed eyes, his expression unreadable.

'I'll show you around,' he said softly, taking her hand firmly in his and ignoring her resistance as she tried to pull away from him. 'Perhaps I should carry you over the threshold,' he added mockingly, a growl of laughter escaping him as he felt her stiffen beside him.

'Don't be ridiculous,' she said irritably, hoping that he had not noticed the desperation in her voice.

'What's so ridiculous about a man wanting to

carry his bride over the threshold of their home?' he drawled sardonically, his shrewd eyes missing none of the emotions that were battling on her face. He was playing with her, Jassy realised angrily, deliberately reminding her of what she had done.

'Please show me round, Max,' she begged, hoping to change the subject. He stared at her for a second then pushed open the beautifully old wooden door.

The hall was light with pale walls and thick Oriental carpets. It smelled of flowers and polish and Jassy was never to forget that moment when she first stepped inside Oakdene. It seemed to welcome her, swallowing her up in its warm and peaceful atmosphere. She felt as though she had finally come home after a long and tiring journey.

The house was furnished perfectly, with both antique and modern furniture, vivid contrasts of shade and colour met Jassy's eyes wherever she looked. The lounge had an open fireplace surrounded by old glowing tiles and carved wood. A wicker basket of logs stood at the side of it. Again the carpet was Oriental, the pale green walls hung with framed photographs and paintings. All the furniture in the room was old, mellow and very comfortable, the only concessions to modern living being the impressive-looking stereo equipment and a television.

Jassy's eyes skimmed quickly over everything, imagining dark and cosy winter evenings in front of the log fire, with snow thick on the ground outside.

The long windows were open leading on to the garden and it was all so beautiful and perfect that Jassy wanted to cry.

Max was standing by the door, still watching her carefully. His jacket was gone and so was his tie, his shirt open at his brown throat and his waistcoat undone. Jassy looked at him, dry-mouthed, his fierce attraction assaulting her senses.

'It's wonderful,' she said huskily.

He smiled. 'You can change anything you don't like,' he said softly, giving her a free rein.

'Did you choose the furniture and the colour schemes?' she asked curiously. Max nodded. 'You have perfect taste,' she complimented, looking away from him, outside, at the bright garden. She had known the answer to her question before asking it.

'I married you,' Max replied, and she could not tell whether or not he was serious.

Next he showed her the kitchen. It too had an open fire and every imaginable modern convenience, carefully planned, to blend easily into the old-world atmosphere of the room.

Jassy gazed at the huge wooden dresser, displaying beautiful china, at the rows of shining copper pans and at the window boxes full of fragrant herbs. It was perfect.

And so it continued, room after room, until Jassy's head was spinning with all she had seen. Behind each door there seemed to be some new surprise that made her cry out with pleasure. If she had been asked to imagine the house of her dreams, she could not have imagined a house more beautiful than Oakdene.

Finally there was only one room left. Max opened the door, and stood back to let her enter first.

'Our bedroom,' he said softly. Jassy swallowed convulsively, squeezing past him obviously. A huge brass bed dominated one wall, in front of huge open windows, the light through the trees outside dappling the old and intricate patchwork quilt. Her eyes registered the dark slatted doors of fitted wardrobes, her heart beating suffocatingly fast as she sought to find the words to tell Max that she would not be sleeping in this room with him.

She sensed him behind her, and her words would not come.

'Jassy,' Max murmured huskily. 'Come to me.'

She heard the faint note of command in his voice, and a strong shiver of excitement ran through her.

She turned slowly to find him staring at her with such hungry intensity that she was transfixed for a moment, before turning away from him again, suddenly finding it difficult to breathe.

Then he was beside her, pulling her round to face him, his strong fingers burning through the thin silk of her dress.

'Let me go,' she whispered desperately, struggling in his grasp.

'I can't,' he said simply. 'I've waited too long for you.'

'No—I want. . . .' She felt panic rising up and making her feel sick. There would be no way she could hide her feelings from him if he became her lover. It would be embarrassing and agonising because he did not love her. He had only married her to get his hands on those damned shares. She would not let him make love to her. Not now. Not ever. She needed strength.

But his hands had become gentle on her shoulders, tracing her delicate collarbone, the long fingers sensual.

'Please let me go,' Jassy moaned, terribly aware that she could not resist him for very much longer. She reached up to push at his wide shoulders. 'I won't let you. . . .'

'You can't stop me, nothing can, and you don't want to stop me,' Max muttered against the golden softness of her hair.

It can't be true, Jassy thought dizzily, I don't want him. But to her horror, the hands she had raised to push him away were resting lightly on his shoulders. She could feel the smooth warmth of his skin through the light material of his shirt. Of their own volition her fingers were shaping and stroking the tense muscles of his shoulders.

Her panic had completely dissolved, the familiar weakness flooding through her limbs, destroying coherent thought, and she was treacherously responding as Max drew her into his arms, his mouth finding hers with bruising need.

He kissed her deeply, parting her lips with devastating expertise, then he lifted her effortlessly into his arms and carried her to the bed. Jassy felt the hard, unyielding strength of those arms around her and beneath her, and looking into his eyes she saw the naked desire burning in their green depths.

It was true, she could not stop him, did not want to stop him, and her fear and panic returned at that thought.

'Max. . . .' she began earnestly.

'Be still, Jassy, I won't hurt you.' His voice was incredibly gentle. He laid her on the bed, then moved beside her, his warm urgent mouth possessing hers before she had time to protest, drugging her, until her need for him flared inside her, out of control, and she wound her slim arms around his neck, to tangle her fingers in the darkness of his hair.

His hands were moving at her back, and she felt the downward slide of her zip. Then suddenly her shoulders were bare, as he pushed the white dress down and off, slowly discarding the rest of her clothes. until she was naked beneath his stroking, seeking hands.

He leaned back then, to look at her, and Jassy moved to cover herself, her face very flushed.

'Don't.' He stayed her moving hands with a husky command, and his burning gaze moved hungrily over her slender white body. 'Dear God, you're beautiful,' he said raggedly, his rare green eyes still devouring her. 'I'm almost afraid to touch you, but

I need you so badly, Jassy,' he groaned, lowering his dark head to find her bruised and parted lips again.

His hands slid over her trembling body, tracing the curve of smooth bare skin from shoulder to thigh. He was breathing heavily, his heart pounding against her aching body. There would be no escape.

'Max, I've never. . . .' she groaned, shuddering as his cool mouth touched her breasts, tasting the soft scented skin, as his lips moved to capture a taut nipple.

He lifted his head immediately, his eyes dark and gentle.

'I know that, child, and I won't hurt you, I swear,' he promised softly, burying his face against her satiny skin.

Jassy could not fight him any longer. She loved him and he had aroused her so expertly, so fiercely, that her only desire was to satisfy the hard need that she felt tautening his powerful body.

She reached for him, fumbling with the buttons of his shirt and finding the warmth of his hair-roughened chest. She heard him draw breath sharply and unevenly as she began to touch him, stroking her small hands over his warm skin to find the muscled flatness of his stomach.

'Max? Are you there?' The low cultured voice of a woman suddenly broke over them as they lay entwined on the huge, sunlight-washed bed. Jassy stiffened.

'Ignore it,' Max muttered thickly, against her bare shoulders.

'Max?' Slow footsteps came up the stairs towards the bedroom, accompanying the questioning call. They both heard them. Max swore long and savagely under his breath, rolling away from Jassy and getting to his feet with lithe angry grace, buttoning his shirt.

Jassy lay dazed, where he had left her, the bright

shadows of the trees outside the window dappling her taut, beautiful body. Max stared down at her with burning tormented eyes, breathing deeply as he regained control.

Then he strode from the room and Jassy was alone. She listened to his low, angry voice outside the door, as she slowly came to her senses. At that moment of realisation she sat bolt upright on the bed. Was she mad? Only minutes ago she had been lying in Max's arms, waiting for his love, and her own weakness disgusted her. She had promised herself that she would not let him touch her, he did not love her after all. She closed her eyes in despair. She had been crazy to go to the register office with revenge in her heart. She would never have revenge on Max, and he would probably destroy her, loving him as she did.

Miserably, she dressed, brushing out her tousled hair vigorously. Who was the woman downstairs? she wondered. Whoever she was, she obviously knew Max well enough to walk into his house and up his stairs in search of him, and Jassy felt a fierce stab of jealousy at this stranger's knowledge of her husband. Glancing at herself briefly in the mirror, she left the bedroom and went in search of Max and the woman.

They were in the lounge. The woman, petite and redhaired and very pretty, was lazing in a chair, casually dressed in elegant riding clothes. Max was standing by the window, smoking idly.

As soon as he saw Jassy he came forward, taking her arm, his eyes still shadowed with desire.

'Jassy, I'd like you to meet Marianne Sargeant, who lives in the village. Marianne, my wife, Jassy.'

'Your wife?' Marianne was obviously taken aback, but controlled her surprise immediately. 'Isn't this a bit sudden, Max?'

'Is it?' Max countered smoothly, his hard face unreadable. The inference of Marianne's remarks was not lost on Jassy.

'How do you do, Miss Sargeant,' she murmured politely, her gentle mouth tightening with an almost instant dislike for this pretty stranger.

Marianne was staring at her, assessing her young beauty with narrowed eyes, as she murmured something equally polite. Her eyes were also noting, with distaste, Max's possessive arm around Jassy's shoulders.

'You're obviously a very clever girl,' she said with a brittle smile, managing to make it sound insulting.

Jassy looked at her, amazed at how rude she was. 'Really, how is that?' she asked blandly. Marianne was not pretty at all, she decided at that moment. She was far too cold and sullen. She was older than Jassy, twenty-eight or twenty-nine. Did she love Max? Had she been waiting for him to propose to her?

'To get Max to the altar, of course,' Marianne replied coolly. 'It must have been quite a fight.'

Jassy gasped. She would not be insulted by this woman, however close a friend she was to Max.

'Aren't you rather jumping to conclusions?' she enquired silkily, a blank smile curving her lips. 'Perhaps I didn't have the trouble that you have obviously had.'

Marianne flushed, and jumped to her feet. 'Are you going to stand there and let her insult me, Max?' she said, turning to the man at Jassy's side, and managing to inject her voice with just the right amount of pain.

'What do you think? You give as good as you get, Marianne, you don't need my help,' Max drawled uncaringly.

Marianne stared at him for a second, then turned

on her heel and left the room. The front door slammed a moment later.

'Bravo, Jassy, you can be quite a little spitfire when you're roused,' Max said softly against her ear. He was obviously amused. Jassy pulled away from him, anger flashing in her brown eyes.

'Did you expect me to stand there being insulted by your . . . your lover?' she snapped furiously, her jealousy still making her nasty.

'Jealous?' Max queried, with mocking eyes.

Her mouth tightened. He was too damned perceptive! 'Hardly. I felt sorry for her,' Jassy lied, her voice flat and convincing.

Max raised his eyebrows. 'Feel sorry for yourself,' he advised softly, laughing at her, his meaning clear.

Jassy flushed deeply. 'You really are the most——' she began, but he cut her short.

'Shall I tell you something, my love? Marianne is not my lover. She is merely a rather over-presumptuous young lady who lives in the village. She was riding past today and she saw the car, so she dropped in, a habit of hers which I don't encourage. Satisfied?'

'I don't care,' Jassy replied stiffly and childishly. 'You don't have to explain yourself to me.' This was another lie. In fact, she felt profoundly relieved that he had. It was so good to know that Marianne Sargeant meant nothing to him—so very good.

Max laughed, his eyes glittering with amusement.

'Perhaps I want to,' he said tolerantly, suddenly serious. Jassy lowered her head, her stomach turning over at something in his voice.

'I'm hungry,' she said, changing the subject quickly.

Max looked at her, his intelligent eyes probing, sensing her sudden withdrawal. 'Let's have dinner, then,' he said lightly. The huge refrigerator in the kitchen was well stocked with food. Max caught her curious glance.

'There's a woman from the village who comes in to clean the place,' he explained.

'Not Marianne?' Jassy teased.

'Not Marianne,' he replied, surprising her by catching hold of her small chin and giving her a brief, hard kiss on the mouth. 'She won't be in to clean the house for a couple of weeks. I've given her a holiday.'

They grilled steaks, prepared vegetables and made a salad together, working in harmony, although Jassy was still avoiding any physical contact with Max. She refused to let her mind dwell on the thought of the coming night, her fear making her a little jumpy.

They ate in silence, and she was aware of the change of mood between them, and Max's eyes resting darkly on her from time to time. When the meal was over and she had washed up, she felt as nervous as a kitten, visibly starting every time Max spoke to her, her answering conversation brief and snappy.

He noted her every action, retiring behind a cool, remote façade, as the evening wore on.

Finally he moved over to where she was sitting and gently touched her hair, a light conciliatory gesture, his mouth thinning as she flinched away from him.

'Okay, Jassy,' he said with cool weariness, 'what's the matter?'

'I don't know what you're talking about,' she replied untruthfully, her heart beating very fast.

'Liar.' You know damned well what I'm talking about,' Max said, sardonically.

'All right—I don't like you touching me,' she retaliated quickly, in a high, nervous voice, her eyes meeting his briefly, then skittering away.

But there was to be no escape, for he tilted her chin with hard fingers, forcing her to meet his enigmatic eyes.

'You haven't been near me all day, you haven't touched me once of your own free will. I want to know why,' he stated flatly.

Jassy stared at him fearfully. It could have been her imagination, but she felt sure that a faint spasm of pain flickered in his eyes for a brief second. Anguish squeezed her heart. She loved him so very much, but he must never know. She had to find some way of holding him off.

'I suppose it's difficult for you to believe that I don't want to touch you,' she said slowly and clearly, retaliating in the only way she could think of, pain clenching inside her like a fist as she spoke so cruelly.

'I don't have to believe it,' Max muttered dangerously, her remark angering him, 'because we both know that it's a lie. Shall I prove it to you?' His hand tightened painfully on her chin and his eyes were bleak with anger as he gazed down at her.

'What, more force?' she enquired scornfully, fear of self-betrayal making her reckless.

'Goddammit, Jassy, are you deliberately trying to annoy me?' Max asked tersely.

'If that will make you let me go, yes!' she almost shouted, feeling desperate and hurt.

'I'll never let you go,' he said fiercely, almost beyond control from her deliberate goading. 'You're my wife, and I want you.'

Despite her struggling protests, he lifted her gently into his arms and carried her upstairs to the bedroom. Jassy fought him every inch of the way, torn between despair and desire, her nails clawing at him, until he grabbed both her small hands in one of his and held them still, swearing violently under his breath.

He deposited her on the bed, then before she had time to scramble away, arched over her, pinning her to the soft mattress.

The weight of his body on hers was weakening her resistance and he was staring at her, holding her gaze with shadowed green eyes.

'Why this sudden change in you, Jassy?' he asked curiously. 'A few days ago, your eyes and your body promised me heaven, promised me everything. I could have taken you any time I chose to, but now——' He broke off, shaking his dark head.

Hot colour stained Jassy's cheeks at his words. Had she given herself away so easily in his arms? she wondered shamefully. 'Now, I detest you,' she said passionately, fighting the deep emotions he aroused so carelessly in her with the only weapons she had left—cruel words. She *had* to stop him making love to her, because she thought she might die of agony if he did.

Max's face closed as she insulted him and she felt him stiffen against her. If she had not known better, she might have thought she had hurt him.

'Now,' he said very slowly, his voice flat, 'you are my wife, and you will have to learn your role as my lover.'

'I wish to God I'd never married you!' she said hysterically, twisting futilely beneath him, hypnotised by the dark, angry glitter of his eyes.

'Well, that's unfortunate,' Max drawled coldly and hurtfully. 'Because I intend to have you—with or without your consent. I have the taste of your body in my mouth, the feel of you beneath my skin, and I'm hungry for more.'

'I'll hate you, if you do,' Jassy warned feverishly, staring at him with wild eyes.

He lifted his shoulder in idle disregard. 'Hate me, then,' he said flatly.

He lowered his head, his warm, angry mouth bruising hers in its ferocity. Jassy lay passive under the hard demand of his lips, but not for long. Her body trembled as she tried without success to evade him, her lips suddenly parting weakly beneath the fierce, persuasive possession of his.

His arms held her forcefully, his hands almost cruel as he forced her to obey him and lie still. She heard him laugh harshly and triumphantly as she acquiesced, and stared up at the face that hovered only inches over hers, at his glittering green eyes, the hard bones of his face, the deep hollows beneath his cheekbones, the hungry, sensual mouth.

She held her breath as his eyes searched hers.

'Did you really think that I wouldn't take what is mine?' he asked with harsh wonder.

Before she could answer, his mouth came down on hers again, different now, the anger and cruelty gone, as he kissed her deeply, forcing her response, a response that she could hold back no longer, when his caressing hands began to move on her body.

She arched herself against the hard, urgent length of him in final and total surrender, her eyes closing and her lips parting softly beneath his, to un- ashamedly match the hunger of his kiss.

He undressed her slowly, touching her shaking body gently, stroking the smooth bare skin he un- covered, exploringly.

Finally she lay naked against him, shivering with need and longing and shyness as his eyes moved slowly over her, brilliant with flame and intense desire. The breeze through the open windows blew cool against her hot face, lifting the tousled cloud of blonde hair across the smooth pillows. She felt no fear as he undressed, but watched every graceful movement of his powerful brown body, with aching attention.

When he reached for her again, she moaned, as their naked bodies came together for the first time, revelling in his strength and his mastery, her arms closing tightly around him, as she felt him shuddering against her.

He aroused her very slowly, his hands stroking over every inch of her. His mouth abandoned hers to move across her throat, her slim shoulders burning wherever it touched, finally reaching the soft swell of her aching breasts.

'Max. . . .' She gasped his name, her fingers clenching against his smooth, unyielding shoulders, her slender white body arching against his mouth, as his cool lips sought and captured a hard nipple, teasing it with his lips and tongue until Jassy was lost in pure sensation, her blood roaring in her ears, deafening any coherent thought.

'Touch me, Jassy, for God's sake touch me,' Max groaned harshly, his breathing forced and uneven as he buried his lean face against her breasts.

Tentatively at first, Jassy did as she was ordered, learning with pleasure how to make him draw breath sharply, how to make him groan as her hands and lips caressed him, the heavy pounding of his heart matching hers.

Her only thought now was to satisfy the aching, thrusting demand of his hard, powerful body, everything else was forgotten, except her own need, her untaught body, shuddering uncontrollably in his arms, almost fainting beneath the sweet torture of his caress.

At last he moved over her, staring down at her with eyes that burned, as they rested on her flushed face.

'Tell me you want me, Jassy,' he demanded raggedly. 'Please.'

'I want you Max, my love,' she trembled, with no thought of denying him.

The fierce and piercing sensual explosion that followed was beyond anything that Jassy had ever imagined, and as Max patiently and expertly carried her to a shattering fulfilment, the last sound she remembered was his deep shuddering groan of satisfaction.

CHAPTER EIGHT

EARLY next morning, woken by the singing birds outside the window, Jassy found herself lying in Max's arms, her cheek pressed to the hair-roughened warmth of his chest, her arms around him.

She lay perfectly still for a moment, listening to the deep, steady beat of his heart, aware that his hands lay possessively on her body. Sweet memories of the night before filled her mind, and flooded her warm languorous body with weakness. She had given herself to him with total abandon, no doubt revealing her love, her need for him.

To him, it would have meant nothing more than the satisfaction of his needs—why should it? She was just another woman, the fact that she was his wife inconsequential. He did not love her.

Despite her efforts to hold them back, her sad tears fell freely over the warm hard body beneath her and she trembled against him, her mind wrapped in grey melancholy.

Max woke slowly, his muscular arms tightening protectively around her as he felt her tears.

'Jassy, what is it, child?' he asked softly, his voice husky with sleep and concern as he tilted up her face to meet his warm, lazy green eyes.

She stared into his heart-stoppingly familiar face with bruised eyes, the breeze from the open window behind them lifting her tousled hair and blowing it across his strong brown throat in a vaguely symbolic gesture.

She shook her head, tears spilling like diamonds

out of her closed eyelids and falling down her pale hurt face.

He watched with inscrutable eyes for a second, then with a muffled curse pressed her shining golden head to his smooth-skinned shoulder, his arms closing around her again.

It was too much to bear, being so close to him, and Jassy struggled desperately to free herself. Max let her go easily.

'Leave me alone,' she whispered, sniffing loudly, and finding herself free of his strong comforting arms, she swung her legs off the bed, uncaring of her nakedness, filled with the need to get away from him. If, as she feared, she broke down and told him of her love, she would be left with nothing, not even her pride.

She looked round wildly for something to cover herself with, desperately fighting the almost overwhelming urge to fling herself back into his arms, to touch his body and beg him to make love to her.

Seeing her fearful, darting glances, Max reached for a shirt that lay within easy reach and tossed it to her, his mouth twisting bitterly as he levered himself on to one elbow and watched her slip into it, her shaking fingers taking ages to fasten the buttons.

'Did you think I was going to jump on you?' he queried softly, his face hard and blank. Jassy flinched, unable to speak.

'I presume that is what this little scene is all about,' he continued, still in that dangerously pleasant voice that grated along her nerve endings.

She could feel him staring at her, but could not turn round. She felt the mattress move and heard the rustle of clothes, and seconds later he was standing in front of her, dressed only in a pair of tight denim jeans that hugged his lean hips and flat stomach.

Jassy met his eyes with a fierce rush of uncontrollable desire weakening her already shaky limbs. In the bright morning light he was magnificent, his overwhelming attraction and his powerful half-naked body leaving her dry-mouthed and breathless.

'Well?' he prompted coolly. Then he sighed. 'Oh, Jassy, what is it? Tell me—I can help,' he said gently.

Self-disgust and bitterness filled her, at her leaping inward response to his voice. This subtle persuasion would not work on her. If he thought he could bully and cajole her into submission, he had another think coming! Her stepfather had tried that too many times for her not to recognise the signs.

'Just leave me alone,' she repeated stonily.

'Is that what you want?' His voice was hard and strange.

'Yes,' she snapped, losing control. 'I don't want you to touch me again, I hate to have your hands on me—I hate you! Do you understand?' She lifted numb, defiant eyes to him.

His face was totally unfathomable, the green eyes suddenly blank. 'You make yourself very clear,' he said wearily. 'Very well, I won't touch you again.' Seeing her disbelieving expression he added flatly, 'You have my word.'

Turning on his heel, he left the bedroom, slamming the door violently behind him.

As soon as he had gone, Jassy covered her face with her hands, shaking reaction gripping her. She could hear Max moving around downstairs—a fair indication of how angry he was, then there was silence.

After crying herself dry and empty, Jassy finally got up and decided to take a shower. Gathering clean clothes together, to lay out on the bed, she was fighting the conflicting emotions inside her heart.

Now that Max had given his word not to touch her again, she was safe. But that did not silence the perverse, nagging voice in her head that insisted she wanted him, needed him to touch her.

What a dreadful mess, she thought wearily as she made her way to the bathroom, her feet dragging lethargically. She showered quickly, then dressed in blue denim jeans and a pale yellow sleeveless blouse, leaving her hair loose.

Apprehension gripped her as she walked silently down the stairs in search of some breakfast, but the kitchen was empty, no sign of Max.

He had made coffee and she poured herself a cup, savouring the rich refreshing flavour as she sipped it slowly. She was not at all hungry, so after washing her cup, she strolled through to the lounge. Also empty. Max must have gone out. A glance through the front door confirmed this, the black Mercedes was not there.

Feeling lonely and deserted, she went back into the lounge and sat down. Max. She longed for him to come back.

At midday there was still no sign of him. Jassy nibbled halfheartedly at a leg of roast chicken she had found in the refrigerator, while gazing out of the window. The day seemed to be dragging by very slowly. With a conscious effort, she pulled herself together. She would not mope around waiting for Max, she would put her time to good use.

A thorough exploration of the house came first. She had found it difficult to concentrate the day before, glancing over the rooms quickly and nervously, beneath Max's intent gaze.

Today she took her time, stepping inside every room and closing the door behind her, her observant eyes missing nothing.

It was another beautiful day, so she opened all the windows wide, leaning out over the sills and looking down into the gardens that surrounded the house.

Reaching their bedroom, she stopped in her tracks, her eyes on the disorderly bed, her face hot. Max's pillows bore the imprint of his head, and she buried her own face against them with an aching heart.

She should collect her belongings and leave now, she knew that, but something strong and unknown held her in this calm and beautiful house, waiting for the return of her husband.

It was ridiculous—to marry a man who she knew was only using her for her body and for what would be hers in two years' time—that had been her first mistake. To imagine that she could wreak revenge on him by marrying him—well, that was laughable! She wondered with a faint smile whether a divorce could be obtained on the grounds of temporary insanity.

But having made all these mistakes, she did not cut her losses and run. No, on the contrary, she stayed in his house, missing him like hell and waiting for him to come home. Perhaps her insanity wasn't all that temporary, she thought wryly.

Life with Morgan, if nothing else, had made her fairly resilient. Max would hurt her, but she loved him, and a shock of insight told her that deep in her heart she still did not quite believe what Morgan and René had told her about him. She was still hoping that he would come to love her.

It was all totally confusing, her emotions were mixed and changing, the only constancy being her love.

Sighing deeply, she got off the bed and tidied it. Memory of the night spent in this bed, in Max's arms, memory of his expression as they made love, would not be driven from her mind, and she felt dizzy with longing for him.

Her suitcases stood on the floor, and the bed made, she decided to unpack them—a small burning of bridges. She peeped inside the fitted wardrobes, finding to her surprise that a number had been emptied for her.

She unpacked her clothes and hung them up, coming across the black silk dressing gown, still carefully packaged. She placed it gingerly on the dressing table, unsure of what to do with it. She could not give it to Max, not now. She remembered how happy and full of hope she had been when she bought it, and her hands trembled as she stored away the rest of her clothes. That done, the room was tidy and her eyes skimmed over it as she stood by the door, her glance falling on a piece of paper that had obviously fallen off the bedside table.

She walked over to it, picking it up absently. It was a folded newspaper cutting and she was placing it back on the table when a name, her stepfather's name, caught her eye.

She unfolded it curiously, her face freezing with shock as she saw what it was—a photograph of Morgan and herself, taken at Kennedy Airport, some years ago. She remembered the occasion well. Morgan had been involved in a controversial land deal at the time and the American press had been waiting for them, hoping for a story, when they flew in late one night.

She read the caption beneath the old photograph without really taking it in, her thoughts chaotic. Then she looked at herself in the photo. She had been nearly eighteen, having just left school, she looked young and tired, her eyes wide and startled.

Why did Max have this cutting? Unless, and she fought against the thoughts forming in her brain, he had been planning this despicable trick concerning the shares for some time. It suddenly struck her that her engagement ring had come in a box from a New York jewellers, so Max must have had it long before he proposed to her. It was too unbearable to think about, and as though the piece of paper was burning her fingers, she quickly opened the small drawer in the bedside table and thrust it inside. To leave it on the top of the table would be to reveal to Max that she had seen it, and she did not want that.

With the small amount of housework done, Jassy found herself at a loose end again. She wandered into the garden, amazed to see a row of beehives in a secluded spot beneath the trees. Homemade honey—her face lit up at the thought. There were vegetables and fruit trees and masses of flowers, just how a garden should be.

She sat down on a tree trunk, lifting her face to the sun. She had never lived anywhere with a proper garden before and it was heavenly just to sit in one as perfect as this. She felt drawn to Oakdene, already she felt as though it was her home.

Damn—her eyes were filling with tears again— why couldn't Max love her?

She heard the telephone ringing from where she was sitting and ran quickly into the house, praying that it would be him. It was Roxanne.

'Hi, Jassy, I hope I haven't called at an inconvenient time!' she laughed.

Struggling with her disappointment, Jassy answered, 'No . . . no, I was in the garden.'

'How are you?' Roxanne asked, her voice sounding overwhelmingly friendly and warm to Jassy.

'I'm fine,' she managed.

'Good. And Max?'

'He's . . . out at the moment, but I'll tell him you phoned. How are you, and Tomás and Rafael?' Jassy asked quickly, hoping that her voice had not given anything away.

Roxanne paused for a second.

'We're all great. Tomás is coming down with a head cold, though—he can't get used to the British climate. Jassy, is anything wrong?' Her concern was almost Jassy's undoing.

'No—there's nothing wrong, why should there be? Please don't worry,' she said hastily.

Roxanne was not really convinced. 'If ever you need someone to talk to, you know where I am,' she said slowly. 'But what I really called for was to ask you and Max for dinner. Some time soon, before we go back to Madrid. Will you come? I realise that it's hardly the time to be asking, you'll want to be alone together, I know!'

If only that were true, Jassy thought sadly, then realised that she had not answered Roxanne.

'We'd love to come to dinner,' she said honestly. 'I'll ask Max, when he gets back, and ring you about the details.'

She felt unsure whether or not Max would want to be seen socially with her, so she could not make any definite arrangements.

Roxanne rang off soon afterwards, and Jassy lit a cigarette from the ornate silver box on the mantelpiece. She had felt like blurting everything out and confiding in Roxanne. Only common sense had held her back. Roxanne was a good and special friend, but she was Max's sister, and they were close. No good could possibly have come out of such confessions.

Glancing at her watch, she saw that it was after six. The afternoon had sped by. She would prepare dinner, perhaps using some of the fresh vegetables from the garden.

As she tied on an apron, she wondered why she could not hate Max when she was fully aware of what he had done and why he had done it. His championship of her against Morgan, she knew now, had been far more personal than she had imagined. It had been nothing to do with her at all—she had even felt that during the dreadful final row at the hotel. Two men fighting for a business, and she had been caught in the middle, a useful pawn. Her stepfather had used her for so long in that role, perhaps it was all she expected. She could not blame Max, she loved him. His intelligence, his strength of character, his gentleness, everything about him attracted her deeply. It was a hopeless situation. Damn him!

She was just sliding a perfectly made beef pie into the oven when she heard the front door slam. Her heart raced away and her whole body tensed nervously. A moment later Max appeared through the kitchen door, taking her breath way, as she looked at him.

He stared at her with unfathomable green eyes, taking in her small bare feet, the apron and her loose golden hair.

'You have flour on your face,' he said expressionlessly. Some greeting! Jassy thought ruefully, wiping her face carelessly with the back of her hand. Max leaned indolently against the door jamb.

'You've missed it,' he said, referring to the flour, his mouth a straight uncompromising line.

Jassy sighed, weakened by his fierce masculinity as he stood there with his arms folded lightly across his broad chest. She strolled over to him, keeping her eyes firmly on his shoulders. 'Show me,' she invited, flashing him a small gentle smile. He hesitated, then reached out, trailing his fingers lightly across her cheekbone.

'It's gone.' His voice was deeper, softer, his fingers not leaving her face but moving, seemingly of their own volition, in slow caress to her small, pointed chin.

His touch shivered through her and she pulled away involuntarily. His mouth tightened. 'More games, Jassy?' he enquired stonily, his meaning crystal clear. She turned away, hurt.

'I've made a beef pie for dinner,' she said in a small voice.

Max raised a dark eyebrow. 'You really are turning into the "little wife", aren't you?' he said bitterly, his voice cold.

Jassy turned on him, her eyes brilliant with unshed tears. 'Yes, I am, but that's what you married me for, isn't it?' she snapped.

'Is it? I wouldn't have said so.' He was infuriatingly cool, angering Jassy further.

'Perhaps it was my business interests that appealed to you, then,' she said furiously, daring him to mention the shares in her stepfather's company.

'Business interests?' he questioned smoothly, his hard face totally blank.

Jassy could have hit him. 'I'm not stupid you know!' she said angrily.

'I never supposed you were,' Max said laconically, his eyes shuttered and bored.

Jassy stared at him; he was very convincing. 'You should have gone on the stage,' she said icily.

Max smiled, his lean face slashed with amusement. 'I don't know what the hell you're talking about,' he said gently, 'but you're beautiful when you're angry.'

Jassy bit back her furious retort, childishly stamping her bare foot as an outlet for her anger.

'You are incorrigible!' she spluttered, her face flushed, her eyes flashing fire.

'So they tell me,' Max said softly, laughing at her.

She turned away and began peeling the potatoes. There was no way she could get the better of him, she thought wearily, nearly slicing off the end of her finger in her frustration. She could feel his eyes on her, watching her every movement, then suddenly he was gone.

She relaxed weakly against the sink, breathless with relief. The vegetables were cooking and the pie in the oven was emitting a mouthwatering, savoury smell—everything was under control, and Jassy decided to shower and change.

She reached the kitchen door and collided with Max. He steadied her, his fingers painful on her shoulders, and it was then that she noticed the box in his hands. It was the dressing gown she had bought him. Her heart sank as she realised that she had left it on the dressing table when unpacking her clothes.

His eyes searched her face, darkening slightly as they rested on her vulnerable mouth.

'For me?' he asked quietly.

Jassy licked her lips nervously. He was standing so close to her that the clean male smell of him filled her head, making her dizzy. His hand still rested on her shoulder. She wanted to lie to him, but found, inexplicably, that she couldn't.

'Yes, it's for you,' she whispered, lifting her eyes to meet his with faint defiance, frightened that he would laugh at her. But his face, as usual, was totally inscrutable as he tore off the festive paper and opened the box. The black silk looked cool and fragile in his tanned hands, a potent combination.

He stared silently at the dressing gown, until Jassy was forced to ask,

'Do you like it?' She could have bitten out her tongue for revealing her eagerness to please him.

'Yes, thank you. I——' He seemed about to say something else, but stopped abruptly, leaning down to kiss her forehead, briefly, his mouth cool and unemotional. 'You're a very thoughtful and generous lady,' he murmured against her hair.

'You're laughing at me,' she accused very quietly, pulling away from him.

'No.' He caught her arm easily as she moved to get away. 'Not at you, Jassy, at myself maybe,' he said with harsh cynicism.

'I don't understand,' she said, meeting his eyes questioningly.

Max shrugged, drawing her eyes to the wide, tanned shoulders beneath his thin shirt.

'Perhaps it's better that you don't. It doesn't matter,' he said dismissively.

Still feeling rather hurt, Jassy moved past him, aware that the conversation was over. He did not detain her and she felt sad that he would not explain anything to her. She had so many unanswered questions.

She ran upstairs to the bathroom and took a quick shower, then after drying her hair and applying a light make-up, looked through her wardrobe for a dress to wear. She finally chose a white cotton dress with a wide flaring skirt, edged with lace. It had a tight camisole-style top, also trimmed with lace, and thin lace shoulder straps which held up the low-cut bodice. It suited her well, giving her pale skin a honeyed sheen. She slipped on her high-heeled sandals, and taking a last check in the mirror, left the room.

Max stood at the bottom of the stairs watching her as she descended, his narrowed eyes examining every inch of her. She tried to ignore the tightening in her stomach as she ran lightly and gracefully towards him. When she reached him, she smiled, unable to stop herself, her mouth a shining invitation.

'How do I look?' she asked, pirouetting in front of

him, urged on by some devil inside herself that she could not control.

'Incredibly lovely—but you know that,' Max answered huskily, his eyes dark and stormy as they rested on her slim bare shoulders and the soft high swell of her breasts, clearly visible beneath the low-cut bodice.

'Do you desire me?' she asked softly, unable to believe her ears as she heard those words spilling unbidden from her lips.

'More than any other woman I've ever known,' Max replied in a harsh, tormented voice. Jassy was shaken by his intensity, and unaware of her own actions, she reached up and traced the firm line of his mouth.

He caught her hand, holding it to his lips as he lingeringly kissed the palm. His touch burned through her, weakening her resistance, as with one sure, fast movement, he found her mouth, kissing her with such urgent savagery that she broke up in his arms, melting against his taut body in submission, her small hands tangling in the darkness of his hair to pull him closer.

A second later she was free again as Max released her so suddenly that she almost fell.

'Max . . .?' She looked up at him, her mouth bruised and swollen from the brutality of his kiss.

He was very still, seemingly calm and controlled, his eyes closed. Jassy looked at the dark lashes against his hard-boned face with wonder.

'Forget it, Jassy,' he advised, his voice dangerously violent, his fists clenching at his sides. 'I have a promise to keep. Remember?'

CHAPTER NINE

Jassy sat in front of the dressing table mirror, carefully examining her face with dissatisfaction.

She had been at Oakdene for a month now, and nothing had changed. Since Max's cold rejection of her on that second day, she had avoided any physical contact with him, even though she lay alone in their huge bed every night aching for his strong arms, his mouth, but more than anything his love. It was tearing her apart, her need for him, and she was unsure how much longer she could stand it. She had lost weight, and her sleepless nights had painted bruised circles around her eyes—she looked a mess, she thought miserably.

It seemed to be affecting Max too, this terrible strain on them both. He too looked leaner, and often weary, his green eyes seemed glazed with dull brilliance. He was unfailingly polite, yet remote, and Jassy's only consolation was the way he looked at her sometimes.

She would catch him off guard every now and again, staring at her with hungry intensity, but his face would close, as hard as stone whenever their eyes met.

The whole situation was downright impossible, and any hopes she might have had that he would come to love her were wearing very thin, and yet she cherished the small things between them, clinging to the occasional warm smile, steadying arm or thoughtful gesture, as a lifeline.

She had lost her heart to Oakdene. It was her home now—apart from which, she had nowhere else to go. As he had promised, Max gave her complete control of the house, and he had also given her a car, a chocolate brown sports car, so that she would not be tied to the house.

He was so very kind and considerate. A week before, he had arrived back from London one evening, with the car full of packages. He had carried them inside, one by one—some of them were very large, smiling enigmatically at her impatient curiosity and refusing to answer her questions. When the last package was in the lounge he had said, 'Open them—they're for you.'

She had opened every one quickly, with excited hands, to find that he had bought her everything she needed to start painting again. Easels and canvas, paints and paper—everything.

She had flung her arms around him, uncaring of rejection, her eyes shining like stars, murmuring her thanks against his mouth. He had not put her away from him, as expected, but had kissed her, briefly and gently, a kiss that she remembered even now for its warmth.

After that, she had begun painting in earnest. Max encouraged her, honestly critical, not hiding his admiration for her talent. She painted the house and the garden, and at the moment was trying to pluck up the courage to ask him if he would sit for a portrait. She longed to paint him, the sharply defined bones of his face and his rare green eyes haunted the artist in her. She must ask him soon.

They had also been to Roxanne and Tomás' house for dinner. It had been a very enjoyable evening. Max had been charming and attentive, giving away no clue that their marriage was anything but perfect. Jassy had almost believed it herself.

Sighing, she began to apply her make-up, concentrating on her eyes, her mind as always on Max.

They seemed to be living in a state of suspended animation and she sensed that the situation would come to a head very soon. Either that, or they would both be driven insane.

There was a certain routine to their lives now. Max would spend the day in London, she would miss him all day and cook dinner for him on his return. On evenings when they had no social engagements, they would sit together, listening to music and talking. Jassy had learned a lot about him. He had told her about the toughness of life in New York, of the travelling he had done, of his business, and she would listen avidly, storing away everything he said, never forgetting anything. He seemed keen to open his life to her and let her get to know him, but even so the barriers between them remained. She slept alone every night, becoming used to hearing the chink of the crystal decanter as she climbed the stairs.

Sometimes Jassy was content just to live with him and see him every day. These were days when she did not care about his reasons for marrying her, it was enough that he let her share his life. On darker days, though, a slow fuse of resentment burned inside her. She wanted to scream at him, hit him, accuse him and beg him to make love to her, anything to crack that cool, distant façade.

As she applied mascara to her lashes, she allowed her mind to touch on her worst and most pressing problem. She was fairly sure that she was pregnant, and if she was. . . . Dear God, she thought desperately, it did not bear thinking about.

She had been sick for two mornings running now, and she could almost feel the changes inside her body, so earlier that afternoon she had made an appointment at the doctor's for the end of the week.

Once she knew for sure, she would have to make

her plans for the future. Knowing that Max did not love her, it followed that he would not be pleased to learn that she was carrying his child. It would not be fair to burden him, therefore she would not tell him, she would go away. Where? How? Her mind buzzed with questions. The clock in front of her told her that she would have to get a move on, or she would not be ready in time.

She outlined her lips and coloured them with soft, rich colour. She had done her hair after bathing, it was looped in a rich shining coil at her nape, the style giving her an air of sophistication. Her dress had been bought by Max, a deep brown velvet sheath, that hugged her slender curves, accentuating the innocent brown of her eyes and lightening her hair to spun gold.

The mirror threw back her reflection and she hardly recognised herself. A slim, poised and incredibly alluring woman with wide, soft eyes and shining hair stared back at her. I don't feel like that at all, she thought wryly, as she stepped into her high-heeled shoes.

A polite tap on the door brought Max strolling into the room. He stared at her with narrowed, appraising eyes, while Jassy stood still, faint colour staining her cheeks. He was looking devastating in a formal black dinner jacket, immaculately tailored to the powerful contours of his body and slim-fitting black trousers. He seemed to fill the room with his aggressive, masculine presence, and the now-familiar weakness tightened Jassy's stomach, as she looked at him.

'You look beautiful,' he said in a voice devoid of expression. He held out a long, flat case. 'These are for you, they'll complement your dress.'

Jassy took the case from him with hands that only shook a little—she had almost learned how to mask the tremulous desire that he induced in her—and opened it, a small cry of delighted surprise escaping her at what lay beneath the lid. It was a fine gold necklace set with diamonds so pure that they seemed to glow with inner fire, the box also containing matching earrings.

She looked up at Max, catching once again in his eyes that fierce hungry look that seemed to set her whole body alight. 'Thank you—they're quite lovely. I think I'll be scared to wear them almost. . . .' she said quietly.

'Why?' He was looking at her with a faint smile on his dark face.

'In case I lose them, they're so delicate.'

'If you do lose them, I'll buy you some more—it doesn't matter,' he replied carelessly.

Jassy frowned. She had not meant him to take her remark that way. She had considered the jewellery a present, but Max made it clear that as far as he was concerned it was merely a pretty investment, and for some reason that hurt. She took the necklace listlessly out of the case, her spirits swooping downwards.

'What's the matter?' Max questioned patiently, taking the shining necklace from her unresisting fingers, his eyes keen and perceptive on her suddenly-sad face.

She shook her head, striving to appear normal. 'Nothing, really.' But the tremor in her voice gave her away.

Max slipped the necklace into his pocket and cupped her face in his strong gentle hands, his fingers absently stroking the soft skin of her cheeks. 'I know you, Jassy, I can read you like a book. There's something wrong and I want to know what it is,' he said firmly, raking her small face with piercing eyes.

Tired of lying, Jassy decided to tell him the truth. It was about time they had a bit of honesty between them, and just at that moment she did not care about the consequences.

'I thought you meant the necklace and the earrings as a present, that's all,' she said carefully.

He looked at her blankly for a moment. 'Would you want me to give you such presents?' he asked curtly.

Jassy turned her face away in silence.

'Well?' he prompted coolly when she did not answer.

'I don't know—probably not,' she lied, meeting his eyes defiantly.

'There's no problem, then, is there?' he muttered coldly, his hard face closing—an expression she was well used to.

'I suppose not,' Jassy snapped, tired of all the bickering, her voice becoming perilously high. 'You're always so damned cold,' she added spitefully.

'That's how you wanted it, if you remember,' Max bit back harshly. He had released her face and now he turned away from her, his eyes distant as he gazed out of the window. 'Can I take it you've changed your mind?'

The bitter mockery in his deep American drawl sparked anger inside Jassy. She was certain that he knew perfectly well how she felt about him, even though she had desperately tried to hide it. He was too intelligent, too perceptive not to have guessed. So what did he want? An admission of love? She stared blackly at his tall, still body, at the proud thrust of his dark head.

'I'll never change my mind about you,' she hissed at him, regretting such harsh words even as she uttered them. Max shrugged, his broad shoulders lifting expressively. 'Why are you so worked up, then?' he asked silkily and so cleverly.

Jassy's whole body slumped. Why indeed? 'You

seem to bring out the worst in me,' she said quietly.

Max sighed, heavily, as if he too was tired, very tired.

'I know,' he conceded, his voice terribly weary. 'And the reverse is also true. Without trying, you can spark off some dark violence inside me—it's crazy!' He paused, coming to rest his hands on her shoulders. 'Jassy, we'll have to talk—soon. This thing——' he raised his hands gracefully in an all-encompassing gesture, 'it's destroying both of us. Day after day, night after night—Goddammit, it can't go on!'

She saw the torment in the depths of his green eyes. Would he tell her to go? Perhaps he had realised that the shares in her stepfather's company were not worth the two years of hell that living with a woman he did not love and could not touch would cost him.

She was suddenly frightened. If she did have to leave Max and Oakdene, she would lose everything.

'We're going to be late,' she said shakily, completely changing the subject, pretending that he had not spoken.

Max noted the panic widening her eyes with a twisting of his mouth, as he glanced at the watch on his brown wrist.

'You're right. If you're ready, we'll go now,' he said politely, a cold, distant stranger again. He did not wait for her, but left the bedroom immediately.

Jassy grabbed her fur wrap with tears misting her eyes, then ran downstairs, after putting on the diamond earrings from the case Max had given her. She could hardly see through the watery mist in front of her. Max was in the lounge, smoking idly, as he waited for her. 'Max, the necklace . . . you still have it in your pocket. . . . I'd like to wear it,' she said in a high and unnatural voice.

He raised his dark brows but did not comment as he reached into his pocket for it. Jassy stared at his strong sensitive hands, desire gripping her so fiercely that she had to bite her lips savagely, hoping that pain would release her from the fever that held her. 'Turn around, I'll fasten it for you.'

He seemed not to have noticed and she did as she was told. His fingers were cool, brushing the heated sensitive nape of her neck as he fastened the gold necklace, and even though she knew how casual his touch was, it shuddered through her.

Max felt her response, unable to help himself as he slid his arms around her narrow waist and pulled her back against him, his mouth warm on her neck. Jassy swayed helplessly against him, melting into his arms.

'I want you, Jass—dear God, how I want you,' he muttered urgently against her ear. 'I've tried, but I can't keep away from you.' He drew a long shaking breath, his hands moving restlessly up her body to cup her breasts with possessive fingers. Jassy moaned softly, arching her body to his hands. She knew how he felt, and he was right, it was destroying them both.

'Max, I . . .' she began huskily, but he stopped her short, releasing her suddenly, as if certain of what she had been about to say, as if certain she had been about to reject him.

He took her hand. 'Let's go,' he said tightly.

They chatted lightly as Max drove towards London, the tension still between them. Then suddenly he dropped a bombshell.

'I'll be flying to New York at the beginning of next week.' He sounded so uncaring and so casual that Jassy could not bear it.

'For how long?' she asked, stubbing out her cigarette with suddenly trembling fingers, hoping that she did not sound like a nagging, possessive wife. What a joke! Hysteria bubbled up inside her at the shock of his news.

'A couple of weeks, maybe longer. I'm not sure,' he answered carelessly, as if the subject bored him. Ask me to go with you, Jassy silently pleaded, but no such invitation was forthcoming. He was probably only going to get away from her, she thought wildly.

The sky was tinged with ominous green, the atmosphere vaguely heavy and threatening. Jassy wound down her window, needing some fresh air. 'It's very close, do you think there'll be a thunderstorm?' she asked brightly.

Max's hands clenched on the steering wheel. He turned his head to look at her and she was shocked by the violence in his eyes.

'More than likely,' he grated, controlling his temper with obvious difficulty.

Jassy stared at him, wondering what was wrong, but not enquiring, in case she brought his wrath down on her head.

The rest of the journey was completed in silence, and Jassy breathed in the polluted fumes of London with distaste, after the pure clean air at Oakdene.

They were going to a party organised by one of Max's business associates. Jassy had been curious about his decision to attend; he usually avoided such social gatherings like the plague, considering them dreary and hypocritical, but she had not asked him why, when he had announced that they would be going.

The Mercedes drew to a silent halt outside the foyer of the smart hotel where the party was being held. Max's hand slid possessively to Jassy's elbow as they entered the hotel. He was behaving like the perfect husband, she thought bitterly, his eyes warm and frankly charming as he bent his dark head to catch something that she said.

He waited for her while she deposited her wrap, tidied her hair and checked her make-up, then kept her close to him, his arm coiled protectively around her shoulders.

She looked around the room, sipping the white wine Max had fetched for her. She knew nobody here. Max introduced her to people who strolled up to talk to him and she reacted politely, smiling as she murmured charming banalities.

It struck her once again just how powerful and respected Max was in business circles. Hard, ruthless-looking businessmen seemed to be falling over themselves to impress him—very subtly, of course, but Jassy was well aware of the undertones in their conversations. She had attended too many similar parties with Morgan not to know what was going on.

She was idly glancing at an interesting-looking painting near the door when a man entered who she knew. She stiffened, her face becoming pale and fearful. It was René Moreau, with a sleek, dark-haired beauty hanging on his arm.

Max felt the sudden tenseness in her, his eyes following hers. 'Ah, your friend René Moreau,' he said softly, not sounding at all surprised.

'He's not my friend,' Jassy said weakly. Then a thought struck her. 'Did you know he'd be here?' she asked, staring boldly into the shadowed depths of his green eyes.

'Of course. I knew exactly who would be here,' he said smoothly.

'You could have warned me,' Jassy mumbled.

'Warned you? Why should I need to warn you? You're my wife, Moreau can't touch you now.'

Jassy was irritated by the smug arrogance in his

voice. 'I didn't want to see him again,' she retorted petulantly.

Max stared at her. 'You don't have to talk to him unless you want to,' he said patiently, his eyes suddenly gentle and understanding.

'Thanks!' Jassy snapped, not convinced. Then suddenly she took his arm, clinging to him in panic. 'Max—Morgan won't be here, will he?' she whispered desperately.

His eyes darkened as he looked down at her, his fingers touching her face very softly. 'I wouldn't do that to you, Jassy—you should know that.' He was speaking the truth and she swayed against him, weak with relief.

'Yes, I do. It was the shock of seeing René. . . .' She was asking for his understanding, his forgiveness for doubting him, and was rewarded with a warm fleeting smile that took her breath away.

Bumping into René was unavoidable at such a small party, and with Max's help, she prepared herself mentally, not knowing what René's reaction would be when he finally did spot her. Their last meeting had been so bitter and angry that she did not know what to expect, and consequently felt a little scared.

Half an hour later, she had been visiting the ladies' room, and was on her way back downstairs to join Max, when she noticed René standing at the bottom of the stairs. His obvious air of impatience told her that he was waiting for his companion, whom Jassy had bumped into briefly in the powder room. Feeling a little nervous, she did not falter, but held her delicate chin high as they came face to face.

'Jassy!' His thin face was wreathed in smiles, and judging by the spirit she could smell on his breath, she concluded that he had had more than a little to drink. 'I had no idea you were here tonight, *chérie*, it's good to see you—you look wonderful!'

Jassy smiled coolly, stiffening slightly as he leaned forward to kiss both her cheeks in the Gallic tradition. 'Is it? Good to see me again, I mean,' she asked, seeing his puzzled face.

'Ah——' Recollection dawned in his eyes. 'Our last meeting. I behaved unforgivably—I don't know what to say.'

He seemed genuinely regretful, but Jassy was still sceptical as she watched him raising his hands in a gesture of despair.

'I presume you've got over me, then,' she said drily.

René laughed, his face a little flushed. 'I have my pride and you gave it quite a beating,' he said, as arrogant as ever.

Jassy smiled. 'Somebody needed to,' she said sarcastically. 'You seem very happy anyway, despite your hurt pride. By the way, who is that beautiful lady you're with?' She was silently congratulating herself as she asked. It had been foolish, as Max had said, to fear this meeting. She should not have forgotten how shallow René was, she could cope with him easily.

'Ariane? We are engaged. She is beautiful, is she not?' He was obviously well pleased with this sudden engagement.

'Yes, she is beautiful—and I assume her father is rich,' Jassy said without malice.

René had the grace to look a little crestfallen. 'I love her,' he said in his usual over-dramatic fashion.

'Oh, I'm sorry—her father isn't rich?' Her face was innocent as she spoke.

René smiled. 'But of course he is.' Jassy pitied Ariane, wondering if she had seen the hard, sullen side of René yet. God help her when she did. 'Marriage would be out of the question, otherwise,'

René added, making it sound like a matter of fact.

'Have you seen Morgan?' she questioned, at last plucking up the courage to ask.

René thought for a second. 'I believe he's in Munich at the moment. He's just pulled off a multi-million dollar deal there. I saw him a fortnight ago—he was very well, as you can imagine.'

'He's happy?' Jassy persisted.

'Did you think he would break up because you walked out on him?' René asked shrewdly.

'No, of course not, I just wondered how he was.' The conversation was beginning to depress her. Why couldn't René answer a simple question? she wondered irritably. She did not need or welcome his opinion on her relationship with Morgan.

'You can rest easy, *chérie*. Morgan is fine. Although you did treat him very badly, you know,' he could not resist adding.

Jassy glared at him impotently. 'That's none of your business, it was between Morgan and myself,' she said, controlling her temper with difficulty.

René regarded her with careless amusement. 'They say the truth always hurts,' he said, with a small smile

'You really are a swine,' Jassy said coldly. He was totally insensitive and cruel.

'What have I done?' he asked, surprised by her vehement remark.

Jassy fumed inwardly at his innocent pretence. What had he done? The list was endless? Although looking at him now, she could quite well believe that he did not know. It was time he found out!

'You've ruined my marriage for a start.' I wish to God that you'd never told me about the shares. But more than *anything* I wish you'd never told me that Max knew about them,' she snapped, her voice weary with bitterness. 'There are things better left unsaid, but you prefer to hit below the belt, don't you? And all for the sake of your pride! Well, I hope you're pleased with yourself—Max and I are finished, because of you!'

This was not strictly true, but something in René's ruthless behaviour, his lack of regret for the bad things he did, had triggered off all Jassy's pent-up hurt and anger, and she wanted him to know exactly how much damage he had caused.

She turned away from him, only wanting to be back with Max, but René caught her arm, detaining her. 'What are you talking about?' he asked, frowning as he stared at her.

She shrugged out of his grasp. 'You know very well what I'm talking about. You came to my hotel the day I got married, or has that slipped your mind?' she said acidly. She was too angry to notice the curious looks they were receiving from people going up and down the stairs.

'I remember,' René said brusquely. 'And Bellmer knows about the shares? You told him?'

Jassy read the shock in his eyes with surprise and impatience. He must have had more to drink than she thought. 'I didn't have to, he already knew—you told me he did,' she snapped miserably.

'I was very angry that morning,' René said slowly, shaking his head. 'Very angry. But there are only three people who know about those shares—Morgan, you and myself.'

'And Max,' Jassy added.

'No. Unless you have told him, he does not know.' René was emphatic.

Jassy put her hand over her eyes. 'I don't believe you,' she said slowly as the implications of what René had revealed sank in.

'Jassy.' René took her hand and pulled it away from her eyes. His expression was sincere and worried. 'You must listen. I don't remember what I said that morning, I was mad with anger, and despite what you think, I do care for you, *chérie*, I've always cared for you. I swear to you that Bellmer did not know about the shares. Do you think Morgan would have let that information leak out? He only told me because he thought the wedding was set up. You did not even know yourself.'

'Why are you telling me all this now?' she asked painfully. 'When it's too late.'

'There used to be an affection between us, *chérie*— oh yes, I know what you think of me, and you're probably right. I am what Papa wanted me to be.' He shrugged. 'It suits me fine. But I did not mean to hurt you Jassy, ever.'

She stared into his face, glimpsing the old René she had known and liked, and she believed him, even though she could not forgive him. 'Thank you for telling me the truth. Better late than never, I suppose,' she laughed, high and brittle. 'Congratulations on your engagement. Goodbye, René.'

'Jassy——' He tried to detain her again, but she walked away, swiftly, back into the noise of the party, feeling worse than she had ever done in her life.

'Where have you been? I missed you.' Max's low, easy drawl hardly penetrated her thoughts, as she got to his side. 'Talking with René,' she answered automatically, her voice deadly.

Max stared down at her probingly. 'He's upset you?' It was more of an angry statement than a question.

Jassy shook her head, looking him straight in the eye. She had to know the truth.

'Do you know that I own shares in Morgan's company?' she asked, carefully searching his lean, beautiful face for signs of deceit. There were none.

'Good for you,' he answered uncaringly. 'Jassy, has Moreau upset you?'

He did not know, he had never known, but most of all, he did not care! Her eyes filled with tears as bright as the diamonds at her throat.

Max saw them, and his body tensed with anger. 'That bastard—I'll kill him!' he grated brutally, his eyes searching the room for René.

'Max——' She laid her hand on his arm, feeling the hard, clenched muscles beneath the expensive material. 'Please take me home now, *please*!' she begged, with her heart in her eyes.

He took one look at her and agreed. 'Okay, Jassy, we'll go now.'

They drove back to Oakdene in silence. Max attempted conversation, but Jassy could not answer him, however hard she tried. She glanced at him covertly, his hard profile unreadable in the darkness, the muscle twitching in his jaw the only indication of his anger. She was appalled at the extent to which she had misjudged him. The coldness and the cruelty she had shown him because of this misjudgment had surely killed any affection he might have felt for her. She had gone too far, and he would never love her now.

If she was pregnant, she would leave him without ever letting him know that she was carrying his child. He deserved to be free of her, free to find a woman he could love. The thought of another woman sharing his life, his love, was unbearable to her, but she had to face it. He had married her because he desired her, because she needed help, and she had learned over the past month how kind and caring he was. For her part, she had thrown that kindness back in his face, denying him her body when she had longed to give it to him.

She only hoped her deep love for him would make her unselfish and help her to give him up.

The car was suddenly lit up by a jagged fork of

lightening ripping open the sky. Jassy looked up in surprise. They were pulling through the gates of Oakdene, home already. She flinched at her own thoughts. Oakdene was no longer her home, she must remember that.

By the time the black Mercedes had pulled up at the front door, the rain had started, pelting the car roof like drumbeats. Max switched off the engine, and turned to her.

'You look exhausted,' he said with a gentle smile.

'It's been a tiring evening,' Jassy replied noncommittally, not meeting his eye.

'I'll make you some hot milk, you look as if you could do with a good night's sleep,' he said, searching her pale, anguished face with concerned eyes. His kindness hurt her more than any physical blow.

'Why are you so kind?' she asked desperately.

Max frowned. 'I've only offered to boil some milk,' he replied drily.

The rain was driving down even harder now, accompanied by deafening claps of thunder and blinding streaks of lightning. Max opened the car door. 'Wait here. I'll open the front door and bring you an umbrella. You're hardly dressed for this.' He slid out of the car, his jacket soaked through before he reached the house.

Jassy watched him go in agony, tears rolling unheeded down her cheeks. It hurt too much to be with him and, obeying her deepest instincts, she slid out of the car and began to run, uncaring of the rain that soaked her to the skin in seconds.

She headed for the trees around the house, where she would be unseen. She had only just reached cover when she heard Max calling her. Ignoring him, she ran on desperately, knowing exactly where she was going. They had been riding together at the weekend and had passed a deserted pavilion near the river. Max had explained that it was due for demolition, after being empty and unused for years. Jassy had been fascinated by its deserted air, the neglected rotten wood of its intricate façade, promising herself that she would return at a later date and paint it.

It took her twenty minutes to reach the pavilion, by which time she was absolutely soaked through, the brown velvet of her dress sodden and heavy with rainwater, and splattered with mud. Cold and shivering with pain and reaction, still tearful, she pushed open the old rotten door which gave easily against her weight, and stepped inside.

It was pitch-black, but at least it was shelter and she was out of the rain. She sank to her knees, giving herself up to the sobs that were racking her body. When at last she could think coherently again, she shifted herself into a more comfortable position on the cold floor, and considered what she would do.

She had been hurt and hysterical when she ran from the car, not thinking, but answering her deep need to get away from Max. Would he be worried? She doubted it. No, that was unfair, he would be concerned for anybody out on a night such as this.

She lit a cigarette from her bag and decided what to do. She would stay here until morning. She had a little money with her, perhaps she would go to Roxanne for help, or Lavender. She would sort something out, because she knew one thing for certain. She could not face Max.

CHAPTER TEN

SHE was dreaming as she dozed uncomfortably. A dark, blurred form was chasing her through equally dark, sinister streets. She could not get away, her feet were heavy and difficult to move, the ground like quicksand, the black, menacing figure catching up with her. She could not see his face, even though the eerie yellow light fell clearly on his moving shape. He was getting nearer and nearer. . . . She woke with a scream, shivering uncontrollably, not knowing where she was, and wondering why she could not see. Of course, she was in the pavilion by the river; she must have fallen asleep.

The rain had still not stopped, it was pelting against the building, and there was another noise. Jassy held her breath, straining her ears to hear. Footsteps coming towards the door—that was the noise. She froze in panic, her heart racing, deafening her, totally paralysed as the door groaned open and the slow footsteps came nearer. A beam of torchlight touched the wall behind her, and she shrank into herself, speechless with fear.

'Jassy, are you in here?' Max's voice, strained and urgent, came to her ears, and she let out the breath she had been holding for so long, on a long moan of pure, shaking relief.

The torchlight caught her, blinding her for a moment, then Max was at her side, swearing long and hard beneath his breath, as he looked down at her, a lost and lovely child in the dim light.

'What the hell are you doing here?' he asked furiously. 'I've been out of my mind with worry!'

Jassy did not answer, could not have answered to save her life. Still swearing, Max reached down and touched her wet cheek. It was ice cold. He bent with fluid, athletic grace and lifted her effortlessly into his arms, and leaving the pavilion, carried her back to the house.

Jassy lay limply in his arms, her head bent to his shoulder, her arms around his neck. 'What time is it?' she roused herself sufficiently to ask.

'After three,' came the clipped and furious reply.

She was surprised. That meant she had been in the pavilion for over two hours. She did not know how, but she knew that Max had been searching for her, all that time. He was as wet as she was, his dark hair plastered to his head, his jaw clenched with anger, as he strode towards Oakdene's welcoming lights. The expensive dinner jacket she rested against was ruined, the material squelching beneath her fingers.

'I . . . I'm sorry . . . for being so much trouble,' she whispered, suddenly shocked at what she had done.

'Be quiet and keep still!' Max gritted in reply, and she closed her eyes at his harshness, doing as she was told.

As soon as they reached the house, Max carried her upstairs immediately, not letting her down until they were in the bathroom. Then he deposited her ungently on a soft, padded chair and began to run a hot bath for her. While he waited for the bath to fill, he stripped off his sodden jacket and rolled up his sleeves. He turned to her, raking her mercilessly with green eyes still brilliant with anger.

'Stand up,' he ordered, in a tone that brooked no argument. Jassy obeyed, struggling to her feet with difficulty, feeling stiff and icy cold. It was only as his fingers found the zip of her dress that she realised his intentions.

'No! I can manage,' she said, panic-stricken, twisting away from him.

His mouth tightened ominously. 'Go ahead, then,' he said tersely, leaning back and folding his arms across his broad chest, watching her.

Jassy shot him a look of pure hatred, before trying to reach the zip of her dress. Her arms were cold and tired and very heavy and she seemed to have no control over them whatsoever. Several minutes of silence followed, as she struggled with the zip, getting nowhere, acutely aware of Max, narrow-eyed, watching her. She had to admit defeat.

'I can't do it. Will you help me?' she begged tearfully.

He reached for her gently, his anger gone, and unzipped the dress, stripping off all her clothes quickly, his attitude businesslike. He helped her into the steaming bath and she lay inert and numb in the hot scented water until she felt some of the feeling seeping back into her weary limbs.

Max knelt at the side of the bath, soaping her body gently, removing the mud that had dried on her, rubbing the life back into her. She coloured brightly as their eyes met, feeling dreadfully embarrassed at her nakedness, but his eyes were blank and impersonal as he loosened the pins in the heavy coil of her hair, threading his fingers through it, before beginning to shampoo it. She felt almost human by the time he lifted her out of the bath and into a thick warm towel.

'Better?' he queried gently, his mouth tender.

'Yes, thank you,' she murmured, still a little embarrassed. He rubbed her dry until she was tingling all over, then he dried her hair and dressed her in a warm nightdress and thick dressing gown.

That done, he sat on the side of the bath, his wet shirt clinging like a second skin to his broad, muscular shoulders, and there was a weariness about him that touched Jassy's heart. She smiled at him, her love for him lighting her shining face. Max caught his breath as he stared at her, his green eyes devouring that smile like a drowning man would devour oxygen.

'Thank you for rescuing me, and all this. . . .' she lifted her small hands expressively.

Max shook his head. 'You're a crazy, beautiful woman and you're welcome,' he said laughingly. Then he was serious. 'What do you want to do now, Jassy. Sleep or talk?'

'Talk,' she answered promptly, knowing that the time had come to clear the air and get things straight between them. 'On one condition,' she added, her face stern.

'Which is?'

'That you get out of those wet clothes and take a bath too,' she said firmly, her mouth stubborn and incredibly lovely to his watching, seeking eyes.

'As you wish, wife,' he said softly, mocking her bossiness.

He shrugged out of his shirt as she watched, and she stared at his powerful, hair-roughened chest with hunger, colouring as he caught her watching him.

'Won't you help me?' he asked in a low voice, his eyes laughing.

'You don't need any help,' she said sharply, fighting her longing to do as he asked. 'I'll make some coffee.'

She turned to leave the bathroom, his voice halting her. 'Jassy, even I need help sometimes,' he said deeply and significantly.

She ran downstairs and into the kitchen and switched on the percolator. It was good to be home, even though her future was uncertain. She strolled into the lounge, switching on the lamps and pulling closed the curtains, these small actions giving her immense satisfaction. The fire was laid, and she put a match to it. The dry, fragrant logs caught fire easily and by the time Max appeared she was sitting on the floor in front of it, her knees tucked under her chin, her eyes faraway and dreamy as she gazed into the flames, the tray of freshly-made coffee at her side. He watched her silently until she sensed his presence and turned, greeting him with a smile. His hair was damp, the dark shirt unbuttoned, and the tight jeans he wore hugged his lean hips and hard stomach. He moved forward and came to sit beside her. Jassy poured the coffee, her hand shaking a little as she handed him a cup, his nearness overwhelming.

Max lit two cigarettes and handed one to her, and they sat in companionable silence for a few moments, until he turned to her.

'Why did you run away tonight?' he asked levelly, his eyes hooded.

It was a question that Jassy dreaded. The time had come to arrange her leaving and it hurt like hell. She was physically aching with her love for him and it was difficult to answer.

'I don't know . . . it was a stupid thing to do—I was acting on impulse. . . .' She broke off with a shrug.

'Do you want to leave here?' His body was suddenly very still and he was watching her carefully.

'No,' she admitted truthfully, lowering her head.

'That's good, because I won't give you a divorce, Jassy,' he warned harshly.

Her head jerked upwards, meeting those fierce, tormented green eyes. 'Why not? It would be for the best,' she whispered, her voice shaking. Best for you, she added silently to herself, her heart breaking to admit it.

'Like hell it would!' Max said angrily, flinging his half-smoked cigarette into the fire in a hard, violent gesture. 'I'm telling you, Jassy—no way. Not now. Not ever!'

She turned away from him, shocked at his insistence that they should stay married when he did not love her. 'You're being ridiculous,' she said quietly and painfully.

He caught her shoulder and hauled her round to face him, the hard, possessive fingers bruising her. His face was a taut mask of fury and repressed violence. 'Am I?' he demanded grimly, shaking her slightly. He saw the fear in her wide eyes, his broad shoulders hunching as he released her. 'Okay, I'm being ridiculous,' he conceded heavily. 'But that doesn't change the fact that I won't let you go.'

'How can you be so cruel?' Jassy cried suddenly, knowing that it would destroy her to live with a man who did not love her. 'You must hate me.' Her voice shook and she was dangerously near to tears.

'Hate you?' His laugh was hard and humourless. 'I could never hate you, Jassy. I love you more than life itself. God, I'll always love you.'

She looked up into his harsh face, torn by the pain in his eyes. 'But how . . .? I don't understand,' she mumbled confusedly.

'What is there to understand? It's simple—I love you, Jassy, and I can't let you go. I thought I could, if ever you wanted to go—but I find I can't—I won't,' he said roughly, pulling her into his arms, his mouth hard and demanding against hers, kissing her deeply and hungrily until she was responding mindlessly, a slow languor warming her body, making her cling to him, her hands touching his hard-boned face.

When he lifted his head and gazed down at her,

she still clung to him, her eyes closed, her lips still parted.

'Jassy, I need you. I know you're too young for me—it's been driving me crazy, but I loved you from the moment I first saw you.' He smiled, seeing her surprise. 'Yes, I fell hard, very hard. It was like being hit by a truck—I've never recovered,' he said wryly.

'On the beach?' she asked faintly.

'Two years before that,' he admitted, shocking her again.

'But I didn't know you then,' she protested in amazement.

'No, but I knew you. I saw a photograph of you and your stepfather in the newspaper. You'd just flown over to the States. Carrington was involved in some shady land deal and the press were at the airport.'

Of course, the newspaper cutting she had accidentally found in the bedroom!

'You attended various business parties while you were over there, and I was at those same parties.'

'I didn't see you,' Jassy cut in. 'I would have remembered.'

'No, I kept my distance, watching you like a love-sick boy.' He laughed. 'I bought the ring the day after I first saw you. You were a married woman, Jassy, from that moment onwards. I meant to have you.'

She stared at him speechlessly, mesmerised by the brilliant, flaring passion in his eyes. Everything was falling into place—the newspaper picture of herself, the New York jeweller's address on the box from her engagement ring—it all fitted. How could she have been so wrong?

'I found out all about you and came over to England to look for a house for you. I knew, just by looking in your eyes, the sort of house you would want. Oakdene was perfect.'

Jassy smiled, delighted with his perception. 'It is perfect. I love it,' she said simply.

Max smiled too. 'I watched you for two years, until I heard the rumour that you were going to marry Moreau. I couldn't wait any longer, so I moved in,' he admitted unashamedly. 'I had intended to wait until you were a little older, but there was no way I could stand back and let Moreau take you. And the more I got to know you, the more I loved you, needed you. I thought that once we were married, I could teach you to love me, slowly, in your own time. I thought I'd have a lifetime to teach you,' he muttered grimly, raking his hand through the darkness of his hair, before continuing. 'I knew you weren't ready to cope with the way I felt for you—you were so young and innocent, I didn't want to burden you with that responsibility. On our wedding night, I lost control, I'd waited so long for you, I thought you were ready, I was angry and I wanted you so badly, I couldn't help myself. When I saw your tears and how frightened you were, I promised not to touch you again—a hell of a promise to keep! I realised that I'd rushed it and I swore that I would wait until you came to me. I'm sorry if I hurt you, honey—I never meant to,' he finished softly.

'Max, I wasn't frightened of you, I wanted you . . . so very badly, but afterwards I thought that it had meant nothing to you . . . I thought you didn't love me,' Jassy said earnestly, needing to tell him the truth.

He touched her golden hair. 'I told you with my body, Jassy, that night. I didn't want to frighten you with words,' he said huskily.

Jassy thought about that night spent in his arms, his gentleness, his patience, his need to give her pleasure before taking his own.

'I know that now. I'm too inexperienced!' she said impatiently.

'That suits me fine—I'll teach you,' Max replied, teasing her and making her colour delightfully.

'You were always so cold to me, and you rejected me,' she said sadly.

Max tilted up her face. 'It was the only way I could keep away from you. I rejected you because I thought you'd hate me afterwards—like the first time,' he explained painfully. 'When I found the dressing gown, it was a ray of hope, it gave me the strength to carry on, night after night, knowing that you were in the next room. Dammit, Jassy, I nearly went out of my mind!' he admitted ruefully.

'Why did you take me to the party tonight, knowing that René would be there?' she asked curiously.

Max shrugged. 'We were getting nowhere together and I began to wonder if perhaps you hadn't known your true feelings for him. It cost me a hell of a lot to take you to that party, there was a chance that I'd lose you.'

Jassy watched the torment in his eyes.

'I don't love René,' she said softly. 'I don't even like him very much. But I have a confession to make about him.' She swallowed, feeling incredibly nervous. Max deserved the truth, and so she began. 'René came to see me the morning we got married. He was angry and convincing. When he'd tried and failed to stop me marrying you, he told me that my mother had left me some shares in her will, that I own fifty per cent of the shares in Morgan's company.'

Max whistled softly, his amazement obvious. 'I'm married to a tycoon, then,' he said with a smile.

'Hardly. Morgan has the shares—anyway, I'm not really interested. René also told me that you had been after a take-over of the company for years, that you knew about the shares and that was the only reason you wanted to marry me.' She paused, her mouth suddenly dry. 'I believed him. I looked at myself in the mirror and thought that you couldn't possibly love me. Nobody had ever loved me, and you were strong and handsome and wonderful, you had your pick of any woman. I misjudged you, Max—I'll never forgive myself for that.'

Max was staring at her intently as if trying to look inside her soul.

'I didn't know about the shares,' he said quietly. 'But about four years ago, I put in a bid for your stepfather's company. I wanted it at the time, but when the deal fell through, I didn't give it a second thought. That's the truth.'

'I know that now. Morgan and René were just trying to pressure me. René told me tonight that he'd lied. That's why I was so upset. I'm so sorry, Max, that I doubted you. It was more to do with me than you. I'd just found out that Morgan had never really cared for me and I felt that nobody ever could.' It was imperative that he understood.

Max smiled very tenderly. 'I do understand, Jassy,' he said softly, reading her mind again.

'Do you forgive me?' she asked tentatively.

He leaned forward and kissed her mouth briefly with warm lips. 'I love you, and there's nothing to forgive. It doesn't even matter now that you know the truth.' He frowned. 'If Moreau told you this tonight, why did you run away?'

Jassy took a deep breath, and dry-mouthed, she whispered, 'Because I love you. I love you more than anything in the world.'

A second later she was in his arms and he was kissing her fiercely and lovingly, and she was matching his ferocity, as they held each other tightly. His warm mouth strayed across her face and she felt him trembling against her.

'Jassy, I've waited for ever to hear you say that,' he murmured unsteadily. 'Stay with me—we'll make a new life together, start all over again— yes?'

'Yes,' Jassy said simply, feeling so happy that she thought she would burst.

'The time for talking is over, I want you now,' he groaned suddenly.

'Love me Max, love me now,' Jassy invited, touching his mouth, her heart stopping at the love she saw in his eyes.

He carried her to their bedroom, laying her gently on the bed, his eyes molten with desire as he undressed her. The sun was rising, lighting the room with a deep glow, as he took her into his strong arms, teaching her love, as his mouth moved on her body. They made love with a wildness that almost destroyed them both, and Jassy moved beneath his urgent body, in ecstasy, feeling the trembling heat of him, filling her, completing her, finally making her whole.

Afterwards, she pressed her face to his sweat-dampened chest, the heavy thunder of his heart beneath her ear.

'Nobody can make me feel the way you do,' he murmured, kissing her hair, his breathing still uneven. Something sparked in Jassy's memory. 'You told me you'd been in love once,' she remembered.

Max laughed lazily. 'I meant you. You're the only woman I've ever loved—ever will love,' he admitted with a smile.

Jassy digested this happily—everything was so perfect.

'And New York?' she asked impishly.

'I wasn't certain how long I could keep away from you. Come with me, Jassy, we haven't had a proper honeymoon yet.'

'Max, I have another confession to make,' she whispered.

His hands slid over her smooth bare skin, possessively cupping the softness of her breasts. 'Tell me,' he demanded gently.

'I think I'm going to have a baby,' she said slowly and clearly.

Max drew a long, harsh breath, freezing for a second. 'Are you sure?' he asked, his green eyes flaring brilliantly with joy.

'I'm fairly sure, I'm having a test this week.' She hardly had time to finish the sentence before she was crushed against him.

'You're so very young. Do you mind?' he asked gently, worried.

'I'm ecstatic,' Jassy replied, kissing him.

'Jassy, my sweet love,' he murmured huskily against the vulnerable skin of her white throat. He touched the soft skin of her stomach with caressing, wondering fingers. 'Our child—in there. I'll make you happy, Jassy, I promise, every single day of our lives. I need your warmth and your softness, your love and your laughter—everything, because God knows, I love you.'

'You have all those things—I'm yours, Max, for ever,' Jassy whispered in surrender against his warm and beautiful mouth.

'Show me,' he ordered huskily, his green eyes glinting with desire as he stared down at her.

It was a command that she could not resist. She would drown him in love. Starting right now.

We value your opinion...

You can help us make our books even better by completing and mailing this questionnaire. Please check [✓] the appropriate boxes.

1. Compared to romance series by other publishers, do Harlequin novels have any additional features that make them more attractive?

   1.1 ☐ yes   .2 ☐ no   .3 ☐ don't know

   If yes, what additional features? _____
   _____
   _____

2. How much do these additional features influence your purchasing of Harlequin novels?

   2.1 ☐ a great deal   .2 ☐ somewhat   .3 ☐ not at all   .4 ☐ not sure

3. Are there any other additional features you would like to include?

   _____
   _____
   _____

4. Where did you obtain this book?

   4.1 ☐ bookstore   .4 ☐ borrowed or traded
   .2 ☐ supermarket   .5 ☐ subscription
   .3 ☐ other store   .6 ☐ other (please specify)_____

5. How long have you been reading Harlequin novels?

   5.1 ☐ less than 3 months   .4 ☐ 1-3 years
   .2 ☐ 3-6 months   .5 ☐ more than 3 years
   .3 ☐ 7-11 months   .6 ☐ don't remember

6. Please indicate your age group.

   6.1 ☐ younger than 18   .3 ☐ 25-34   .5 ☐ 50 or older
   .2 ☐ 18-24   .4 ☐ 35-49

Please mail to: Harlequin Reader Service

In U.S.A.   In Canada
1440 South Priest Drive   649 Ontario Street
Tempe, AZ 85281.   Stratford, Ontario N5A 6W2

Thank you very much for your cooperation.

There is nothing like...

Harlequin Romances

The original romance novels!
Best-sellers for more than 30 years!

FREE!

A hardcover Romance Treasury volume containing 3 treasured works of romance by 3 outstanding Harlequin authors...

...as your introduction to Harlequin's Romance Treasury subscription plan!

Romance Treasury

...almost 600 pages of exciting romance reading every month at the low cost of $6.97 a volume!

A wonderful way to collect many of Harlequin's most beautiful love stories, all originally published in the late '60s and early '70s. Each value-packed volume, bound in a distinctive gold-embossed leatherette case and wrapped in a colorfully illustrated dust jacket, contains...

- 3 full-length novels by 3 world-famous authors of romance fiction
- a unique illustration for every novel
- the elegant touch of a delicate bound-in ribbon bookmark... and much, much more!

Romance Treasury

...for a library of romance you'll treasure forever!

Complete and mail today the FREE gift certificate and subscription reservation on the following page.

Romance Treasury

An exciting opportunity to collect treasured works of romance! Almost 600 pages of exciting romance reading in each beautifully bound hardcover volume!

You may cancel your subscription whenever you wish! You don't have to buy any minimum number of volumes. Whenever you decide to stop your subscription just drop us a line and we'll cancel all further shipments.

FREE GIFT!
Certificate and Subscription Reservation

Mail this coupon today to
Harlequin Reader Service

In the U.S.A.
1440 South Priest Drive
Tempe, AZ 85281

In Canada
649 Ontario Street
Stratford, Ontario N5A 6W2

Please send me my FREE Romance Treasury volume. Also, reserve a subscription to the new Romance Treasury published every month. Each month I will receive a Romance Treasury volume at the low price of $6.97 plus 75¢ for postage and handling (total—$7.72). There are no hidden charges. I am free to cancel at any time, but if I do, my FREE Romance Treasury volume is mine to keep, without any obligation.

NAME _____
(Please Print)

ADDRESS _____

CITY _____

STATE/PROV. _____

ZIP/POSTAL CODE _____

Offer expires February 28, 1983
Offer not valid to present subscribers.

TR208